## MONTANA MAVERICKS

*Welcome to Big Sky Country! Where free-spirited men and women discover love on the*

*LEGACY OF TENACITY*

As the town begins to heal from its scars and scandals, its single cowboys (and cowgirls) are ready for a fresh start. They know that love can grow in the most unexpected places and that down doesn't mean out. So make a wish on a Montana moon for all to be revealed—they've waited for their sweethearts long enough!

*MY HEART BELONGS TO THE MAVERICK*

People are literally lining up to get a smooch from Ryder Trent, Tenacity's "kissin' cowboy." Sure, it's all for charity, but Ella McIntyre knows that Ryder's flirty reputation is well deserved. He is the very last man who should be inhabiting the shy librarian's dreams—or her bed. But she may be the only one who sees past his pretty face and values Ryder for the man he is inside...

Dear Reader,

*My Heart Belongs to the Maverick* is my first time writing in the Maverick world. I hope you like my interpretation of these characters and the Montana setting of Tenacity. I was happy to include Harley, a German shepherd who's retired from the military, in the story. If you've read some of my other stories, you know I love adding dogs to the mix. This time I also added an opossum. Yes, there's a wild Virginia opossum (Didelphis virginiana) in the story. I came to enjoy this highly underappreciated wild animal when one started visiting my deck at night. I have been putting out apple pieces, grapes and banana slices, so he and some friends are now nightly visitors.

I also had fun with Ella and Ryder putting together a carnival combining Valentine's Day and Friday the 13th to raise money for the local library. And guess what? They had so much fun they ended up falling in love. They didn't go easily into that happily-ever-after, so you'll have to read the story to find out how it all ended up. But I will give you a hint. I adore happy endings!

I love hearing from my readers, so be sure to let me know what you think at authorcarrienichols@gmail.com.

Happy reading!

*Carrie*

# MY HEART BELONGS TO THE MAVERICK

CARRIE NICHOLS

MONTANA MAVERICKS

Special thanks and acknowledgment are given to Carrie Nichols for her contribution to the Montana Mavericks: Legacy of Tenacity miniseries.

Recycling programs for this product may not exist in your area.

ISBN-13: 978-1-335-54087-4

My Heart Belongs to the Maverick



For questions and comments about the quality of this book, please contact us at CustomerService@Harlequin.com.

Harlequin Enterprises ULC
22 Adelaide St. West, 41st Floor
Toronto, Ontario M5H 4E3, Canada
www.Harlequin.com

HarperCollins Publishers
Macken House, 39/40 Mayor Street Upper,
Dublin 1, D01 C9W8, Ireland
www.HarperCollins.com

**Printed in Lithuania**

**Carrie Nichols** grew up in New England but moved south and traded snow for central AC. She loves to travel, is addicted to British crime dramas and knows a *Seinfeld* quote appropriate for every occasion.

A 2016 RWA Golden Heart® Award winner and two-time Maggie Award for Excellence winner, she has one tolerant husband, two grown sons and two critical cats. To her dismay, Carrie's characters—like her family—often ignore the wisdom and guidance she offers.

**Books by Carrie Nichols**

***The Fortunes of Texas: Fortune's Secret Children***

*Fortune's Faux Engagement*

***Montana Mavericks: Legacy of Tenacity***

*My Heart Belongs to the Maverick*

**Harlequin Special Edition**

***Small-Town Sweethearts***

*The Marine's Secret Daughter*
*The Sergeant's Unexpected Family*
*His Unexpected Twins*
*The Scrooge of Loon Lake*
*The Sergeant's Matchmaking Dog*
*The Hero Next Door*
*A Hero and His Dog*
*His Unlikely Homecoming*

***Finding Forever in Sandy Shores***

*A Hero's Return*

Visit the Author Profile page
at Harlequin.com for more titles.

This is dedicated to my online sprint-writing friends who keep me sane and writing: Aleks, Lucy, Traci, Jess, Pippa, and Rachael.

# *Chapter One*

"Oh, Ella, you would've loved it. The place was old and drafty."

"Gee, thanks." Ella McIntyre laughed at her friend Cassie's description of the B&B Cassie and her fiancé, Graham Callahan, had gone to recently for a weekend getaway.

"You know what I mean. If you'd been there, you would have been using words like *quaint* and *romantic* to describe it," Cassie continued, tilting her head to the side as if considering something. "Huh, are you sure you didn't write their marketing brochure?"

Ella didn't take offense. As much as she tried to deny it, she knew everyone in their small town of Tenacity, Montana, had her pegged as a hopeless romantic.

Ella sighed. "Sorry. I thought it sounded like the kind of place that—"

"Hey." Cassie lightly touched Ella's arm. "I'm just giving you a hard time. I confess, we had the most wonderful time."

"You're sure?" Ella asked. When she'd seen the brochure for the B&B, she'd thought it sounded like the perfect place for a romantic getaway. Not that *she'd* been planning any. Working at the Tenacity Public Library plus two other places hardly left time to date. But she'd remembered seeing the brochure when Cassie had said she and Graham had wanted to get away for a weekend. So she'd mentioned the place to her friend.

Cassie grinned. "And drafty was the perfect excuse to cuddle."

"As if you two needed an excuse," Ella teased, scooping up returned books from the cart so she could reshelve them. Her boss, head librarian Millie Griswold, had the day off and Ella wanted everything shipshape before she left.

"It *was* wonderful." Cassie sighed. "And yeah, it was romantic, if you get my drift."

Ella pushed a tattered copy of a best-selling romantic suspense back into an empty slot. She tamped down any feelings of envy that threatened to rise up. It wasn't Cassie's fault Ella had no time for a personal life, let alone time for getaways, romantic or otherwise. "Well, I'm glad the place worked out and that you two, uh, made the most of your weekend."

"Oh, we sure did. Barely left the room." Cassie heaved a sigh and stared off into space.

Ella fumbled the two books she'd reached for on the cart. "Cassie!"

"Look at you blushing." Cassie playfully elbowed Ella. "People might think you're a virgin."

Ella silently cursed her fair skin and her inability to control her reactions in situations like this.

"You're not, are you?" Cassie asked, glancing around checking for any patrons in their vicinity.

"Get real. I'm twenty-seven years old, for crying out loud." Ella rolled her eyes, sidestepping Cassie's question. And in the strictest sense, she wasn't a virgin. But she considered that a technicality. Not that she would mind getting more experience. Ha, even if she had the time, the single guys in Tenacity weren't exactly lining up with offers.

*Their loss*, she thought and pushed the cart to the next bookshelf.

"You said you stopped by yesterday," Ella said, hoping to change the subject. She pulled a few more books off the cart. "Did you need something?"

"I did and was surprised the library was closed. I thought it was open on Wednesdays," Cassie said, following Ella as she continued to return books to the shelves.

Ella frowned and shelved another one. "Yeah, we had to cut hours again. Not only does our budget keep shrinking, but we had to pay for repairs to the heating unit. I just hope we don't have to close permanently."

She sighed and glanced around the space that meant so much to her. The interior of the building retained much of its original features, including Tuscan columns, pilasters and two brick fireplaces.

For Ella, this wasn't just a job—it was a calling. Her dream job ever since she'd first walked into the building as a child, holding her mother's hand, awed by seeing so many books in one place. Books were her passion, so it stood to reason she'd consider the library a magical place.

Today, the historic single-story 1909 brick building was a sanctuary for community members: children discovering their first chapter books, seniors researching family histories, students finding quiet study spaces. Each book, each shelf represented connection, knowledge, hope. At least that's what she'd been telling the people who held the purse strings. Not that the funding challenges were their fault. Tenacity, like its residents, was barely scraping by, at least until the dinosaur dig could get underway and the Tenacity Dinosaur Center and Park could start helping the town's economy more.

"Oh no. Is closing a real possibility?" Cassie tsked her tongue. "Don't the people in charge understand how much the people in Tenacity need this place? If you're forced to close, the kids will lose Story Time and the older folks will miss things like those computer classes you offered a few months ago."

Ella nodded. "I'd hate to lose my job, but it's more than that. Like you said, people of all ages would lose out. A lot of them can't make that trip to Bronco. Especially in bad weather."

"Which is like…all winter," Cassie added dryly.

"Exactly," Ella agreed.

"So, what can we do?" Cassie asked.

Ella shrugged. "Well, there's not much we *can* do. Unless someone can come up with a pile of money to throw at the problem, and that's not likely to happen in Tenacity. We might be big on helping one another, but let's face it, we're all a bit short on extra cash."

Ella herself was working two, sometimes three, jobs to make ends meet. As much as she loved Tenacity, she also needed to be a realist. But she wasn't ready to give up yet, no matter how much her parents urged her to move to "someplace with a decent library," as they put it. If push came to shove, she might have to, but she wasn't ready to throw in the towel yet.

"Wait a minute." Cassie's eyes widened and she snapped her fingers. "I think you've come up with a solution."

"I have?" Shelving a few more books, Ella glanced at her friend with a puzzled frown. What in the world did she say that was so inspiring?

"You have! You're right that no one person alone can help. So we appeal to the entire town, involve as many people as possible."

"How do we do that?" Ella asked.

"It's simple." Cassie spread her arms in an all-encompassing gesture. "We plan something for everyone."

"You mean like a bake sale or something?"

Cassie laughed. "I don't think we can bake that many cookies. What about a dance?"

"We can't compete with the town's annual Valentine's dance. Not to mention the upcoming masquerade ball at the Dinosaur Center." Ella shook her head. But her friend's enthusiasm, as usual, was contagious

"We won't. We'll plan something else. Something to include everyone, not just couples looking for a little romance for Valentine's Day."

Ella's growing enthusiasm started to waver. All ages used the library and its services. But what could they possibly do to please everyone? "Like what?"

"What about a carnival? That way people can bring their kids. We'll call it a Valentine's carnival and charge a nominal fee or ask people to pay what they can afford. I think people would be willing to pay a fair amount if they knew it was to keep the library open."

"When and where would we hold it?" Maybe Cassie was on to something.

"Here on the day before. Valentine's Day is on a Saturday this year, so we could hold it on the Friday before so it wouldn't be a school night."

"I like that idea and— Oh."

"What?"

"That means it would be on Friday the thirteenth."

Cassie laughed. "Perfect. We can combine horror and romance."

"What a combination," Ella said, shaking her head.

"Hey, it will get people interested in our carnival."

"How do you propose we pull this off?"

"We'll think of something," Cassie said, waving her hand as if it were of no consequence.

"Cassie, do you know what the date is today? How are we supposed to get all this done in just a couple of weeks?"

"I'll help."

Ella turned in the direction of the voice. She recognized one of the young mothers who brought her son to Story Time. "You're Craig's mom. Heather?"

The woman nodded. "I'm sorry for eavesdropping, but I just don't know what I'd do without this place. We can't afford to enroll Craig in any preschool-type activities. Bringing him to Story Time is the highlight of our week. And I couldn't afford to buy him all the books he loves to read. I know all mothers think their child is the smart, but Craig really is. His curiosity is endless."

"I really appreciate your offer, but I'm not sure that—" Ella began.

"Heather, could you get other mothers to help?" Cassie interrupted.

The other woman nodded. "I know of some that are fabulous bakers, and a friend of mine is awesome at face painting, if you want to set up something like that for the kids."

Cassie turned back to Ella with a big grin. "See? We got this."

Ella knew when she was beat, and the more they talked with Heather, the more the idea took shape. And that Friday night before Valentine's Day was a perfect time. Ella knew that the usual celebrations could exacerbate that feeling of being left out if you weren't in a relationship. She started to warm to the concept, seeing potential where she'd initially seen obstacles, and her skepticism evaporated. "Okay. You've convinced me. I can't stand around and do nothing while the library slips away."

Cassie gave Ella a fist bump and smiled at Heather. "Thanks."

The other woman nodded. "I've got to run. I have an appointment, but…" She pulled a piece of paper and pen from her purse and scribbled something on it. Handing it to Ella, she said, "Here's my number. Give me a call later today or tomorrow. I'll get started rounding up some other mothers to volunteer. I can make a list of what sort of things they can do or are willing to provide. I know I can't be the only one who feels this way."

"That's great. Thank you so much." Ella watched Heather and her son leave. She was happy to be taking action to keep the library afloat. Still, there was that voice in her head that kept asking, *What have you gotten yourself into?*

"It's gonna be fine. You'll see." Cassie bumped shoulders with Ella.

"It's better than doing nothing, I guess."

Cassie drew in a sharp breath, and Ella got a bad feeling in the pit of her stomach. "What?" she asked.

"I just realized the thirteenth is also Galentine's Day."

Ella groaned. "Isn't that a made-up holiday created by a fictional character?"

"Aw, c'mon. It's a real thing *now.* Besides, Leslie Knope is part of pop culture," Cassie said, referring to the character played by Amy Poehler on the television show *Parks and Recreation.*

Ella closed her eyes and shook her head. "Can't fight City Hall. Or you."

"That's the spirit," Cassie said cheerfully and handed Ella a book to be shelved.

"It's my understanding that Galentine's Day is to celebrate women's friendships." Ella slipped the book into an empty slot. "Will that even fit into what we're planning? That's a stretch from Friday the thirteenth."

"We wanted something that fits everyone. Friday the thirteenth can be for the younger set, male and female, and Galentine's will be for the women of Tenacity. Paired or single." Cassie's eyes widened as she picked up a tattered paperback off the cart. "Ooh..." Waving it around, she said, "This! We'll do this."

Ella peered at the book cover and frowned. "You've got to be kidding me. I don't know about this..."

"Where's your sense of adventure?" Cassie asked and handed Ella the copy of the young adult romance *The Kissing Booth*.

"Right next to my sense of self-preservation. I haven't even run the idea of a carnival past Millie. Now you want to add a kissing booth?" Shaking her head, Ella handled the book as if it were a live grenade.

Millie Griswold was technically Ella's boss because she still held the title of head librarian but she was looking toward retirement and had almost completely turned the running of the library over to Ella, giving Ella more hours than Millie herself worked.

"A kissing booth would be a great feature for the Galentine's Day part of our carnival." Cassie laughed. "I remember playing spin the bottle at Danny Sullivan's twelfth birthday party. You must remember that, Ella. You were there."

"Vaguely," she said and joined in the laughter, hoping hers didn't sound as forced as it felt. Her kissing *partner* had been Tommy Keene. He'd been wearing his Coldplay T-shirt and her new braces had caught his lip, making him bleed on his beloved new shirt. She still blushed and had to resist the urge to apologize whenever she ran into him in town. He was now happily married and the father of two boys, so at least she hadn't scarred him for life. No, she reserved things like that for herself. No wonder she was still practically a virgin.

"Earth to Ella."

Ella blinked at Cassie, who was busy waving a hand in front of her face. "What?"

"Thought I'd lost you there for a minute," Cassie said. "Was your first kiss that memorable?"

Ella rolled her eyes. "Yeah, right. I hope you're not suggesting we play spin the bottle."

"No. But what about…" Cassie snapped her fingers and frowned at Ella's expression. "What?"

Ella sighed. "Whenever you snap your fingers, I end up in some sort of scheme."

"Schemes they may be, but you have to admit they're *well-meaning* schemes. We are trying to save your library with this one."

"It's not *my* library. It belongs to everyone in Tenacity."

"Semantics. Now, where was I? Ah, yes. We should get a cover model for the kissing booth."

"Cover model?"

"You know, like in these romance novels." Cassie pointed to the shelves of romance novels as if channeling Vanna White.

Ella chuckled. "I have a feeling that would eat into our profits."

Cassie snapped her fingers again and Ella groaned. What big idea did her friend have now?

"He's not a cover model, but…"

Ella frowned. "Who? Or shouldn't I ask?"

"Like I said, he's not a cover model, but he could be." A mischievous glint appeared in Cassie's eyes. "Yup, perfect."

Ella resisted the urge to stamp her foot. “Who?”

“My brother Ryder,” Cassie said with a satisfied smile. “Yup, he’ll do nicely.”

*Ryder Trent.* Ella knew him only by reputation. He was the closest thing Tenacity had to a playboy. Cassie even talked about his “flavor of the week” at family gatherings.

*You have to admit he’s hot*, that voice inside Ella’s head reminded her, but she wasn’t going to say *that* to her friend. Nor was she going to tell her friend that her idea was simultaneously ridiculous and brilliant. “I don’t know...”

“Trust me, every woman in Tenacity would line up for a chance with the Kissin’ Cowboy.”

Ella raised her eyebrows. “You want to call it ‘Kissin’ Cowboy’?”

“Catchy, right?” Cassie grinned.

“That’s one word for it.”

“Sense of adventure, remember?”

“Sorry, missing in action. I think my common sense is filling in,” Ella told her. It wasn’t as if she didn’t want this to work. She did. She really, really did. Keeping her job and keeping the library open was her goal.

“Remember, Tenacity isn’t just a town name—”

“It’s what we do,” Ella finished for her and chuckled. She didn’t mean to be a wet blanket regarding Cassie’s plans. She was really grateful to her and to people like Heather for their enthusiasm. Saving the library was her main concern, but she also knew it would be an uphill battle. Tenacity didn’t slide into decline overnight, and one night wasn’t going to solve all the library’s problems. But if they could keep it open until the Tenacity Dinosaur Center was up and running, the town's money woes might be a thing of the past.

She still wasn't convinced about this kissing booth idea, either. "What about Ryder? Will he agree to this?"

"Of course he will." Cassie nodded and smiled. "He'll probably jump at the chance."

"You want me to do what? Have you lost your mind?" Fisting his hands on his hips, Ryder Trent stared at his youngest sister. Surely he'd misunderstood her. Where had she gotten a harebrained scheme like that? And what did kissing strangers have to do with keeping the Tenacity library open? "What made you even volunteer me for this nonsense?"

"Don't be such a prude." Cassie swatted him on the upper arm. "You're the one who has dated every single woman in a fifty-mile radius."

"That's a gross exaggeration."

Cassie raised an eyebrow. "Is it? You've left a string of broken hearts up and down Central Avenue."

"Hardly," he scoffed. "They all know up front that I'm not the forever kind. They knew what they were getting into."

He frowned. If he'd broken anyone's heart, it was unintentional. "No commitment" was Ryder's number-one rule. Ever since Janelle had broken his heart when she'd laughed at his proposal, saying she wouldn't be tied to a *hayseed* who was content to live in Tenacity for the rest of his life. What was so—

"So you'll do it?"

Cassie's question broke into his brooding and he frowned. "Again, I ask, whose idea was this? And more importantly, why?"

"I was trying to help Ella," Cassie said in a defensive tone.

"Ella?" Ryder was trying to place the name with a face.

"You know, Ella McIntyre. She's the librarian."

"You mean to tell me she suggested this?" He found the whole thing unbelievable.

"Well, technically, I suggested it to her, but she's very excited about the whole thing," Cassie said, her cheeks pink.

"I find that hard to believe." What exactly had gone on at the library this afternoon?

"Why is it so hard to believe? We want to have a carnival to help raise money to keep the library open. Ella is very dedicated to her job."

Was Cassie being intentionally dense? There had to be a component he was missing. "You mean to tell me that white-haired lady with the orthopedic shoes suggested a carnival with a kissing booth?"

"What are you on about? I'm talking about— Oh! No, that's Millie Griswold with the shoes. I'm talking about Ella McIntyre. Long, wavy blond hair, blue eyes, looks like she could be a country music star with her denim blouses, billowy skirts and—"

"Sexy red cowboy boots," Ryder finished for her and regretted it immediately. Not the boots part, but the sexy part. The way Cassie was looking at him told him he'd made a tactical error. He didn't know anything about her at the time, but he'd noticed this Ella McIntyre going into the library. He'd been in town to pick up an order at Tenacity Feed and Seed and didn't have time for a detour into the library. But he'd been tempted to follow her like she was the Pied Piper.

"Don't get any ideas about Ella," Cassie warned him as if she'd read his mind.

He laughed. Maybe she had. Cassie did know him quite well. He threw his arm around his sister's shoulder. "Why? Is she married?"

"No. Now about—"

"Engaged?" He hugged Cassie closer.

She tried to shrug off his arm. "No, but—"

"Involved with anyone?"

She poked him in his side and he grunted.

"Look, will you do this or not?" she asked.

"Will I get to kiss the librarian?"

"I'm sure Millie would—"

"I'm talking about Ella. Ella of the red boots."

She wriggled out from under his arm. "You'd have to ask her. She may not be willing to pay for that, um... privilege."

"Privilege, huh? You know, for someone who wants a favor, you're pushing your luck, little sister."

Ryder wasn't about to admit to anyone, least of all Cassie, that the idea of getting to know Ella the librarian appealed to him. Some instinct warned him that following that path might not be a good idea, but he was hearing that magical flute that he couldn't refuse.

# *Chapter Two*

Ella adjusted her glasses and smoothed down her flouncy denim skirt for the third time in five minutes. She tucked a few wayward strands of her wavy blond hair back into the sensible bun she'd arranged that morning before leaving home. Her fingers lingered on the bun. Why had she worn it like that today? She sighed. What had she been thinking? She should have left—

The library's front door swung open, bringing with it a gust of frigid February air and the two visitors she'd been nervously anticipating.

Cassie strode in first, bubbling with her usual enthusiasm and natural warmth. Her brother Ryder, whose reputation preceded him like a Hollywood legend, trailed behind. Stepping into the entry vestibule, he removed his Stetson by the crown and held it close to his right side.

"Sorry if we're late," Cassie said. "Ryder insisted on dropping Harley off first."

Ella tried not to stare at the man standing next to her friend. His dirty-blond hair tousled by the removal of his hat, Ryder Trent was over six feet of muscled strength. Dressed casually in jeans, scuffed dark brown

Roper boots and a shearling-lined leather bomber jacket, he looked like the ultimate cowboy.

"In case you'd forgotten, it's February. In Montana," Ryder groused, stepping forward to stand next to Cassie. "I'm sure Miss McIntyre agrees with me that it's too cold to stay outside. Right?"

Ella tried to draw in enough air to speak, but all she could manage was to imitate the Jane Austen bobblehead doll she kept on her desk.

"Harley and I thank you, Miss McIntyre," Ryder said in a rich baritone, a hint of mischief in his dark blue eyes.

God, he was gorgeous. Ella touched the underside of her chin to be sure her jaw was closed as her mind raced. Who was Harley and what was going on? *Harley* was one of those gender-neutral names. Was she a current girlfriend? If so, what did this Harley think about Ryder manning a kissing booth?

Did Ella know anyone of either gender named Harley? No, but Ryder was six years older and they'd never traveled in the same circles anyway. Tenacity might be small, but evidently not small enough. Whoever she was, she was one lucky woman.

Cassie rolled her eyes dramatically and elbowed her brother. "Oh for heaven's sakes, Harley is a German shepherd."

"Oh, did I forget to mention that part?" Ryder focused his attention on Ella and winked, his deep blue eyes reminding her of the leather-bound classics on the library's special collections shelf.

"Let's get this meeting back on track before Cassie derails it," he said.

"Me?" Cassie put her hands on her hips.

Ignoring his sister, he turned his attention to Ella. "Hi. I'm Ryder Trent. And of course you're Ella McIntyre."

He moved his hat to his other side and held out his hand toward Ella. She stared at his outstretched hand for a moment, trying to remember what she was supposed to do. *Shake it!* Yes, that's what she was supposed to do. The calluses on his hands were testimony to the life of a rancher. She missed the skin-to-skin contact when he withdrew his hand. *Don't get any ideas*, she cautioned herself. Ryder Trent was out of her league and even more so up close.

"I, um…yes, McIntyre. Ella. Ella McIntyre." *Brilliant, Ella. Tell him your name twice. Not awkward at all.* "You have a dog?"

"Actually, I'm taking care of him as a favor to my other sister, Renee. Do you have any sisters, Ella?"

She shook her head. His smile widened, and a dimple that should be outlawed in all fifty states appeared in his left cheek. Ella forgot how to breathe.

"Good for you. They just get you into all sorts of *situations*." He emphasized the last word and glanced at Cassie.

"Hey, this is for a good cause. You'll be doing a big favor for everyone who loves this library by helping it to stay open," Cassie told him.

"How do you figure that?" he asked.

"Women will be lined up waiting for a chance to lock lips with the Kissin' Cowboy."

"Kissin' Cowboy?" His handsome face wore a

pained expression. "You've got to be kidding me. How will that help save the library?"

Ella jumped in to try to smooth things over. Sure, she'd been skeptical at first, but after reading this morning's budget report, she was desperate. Even Millie had agreed to the kissing booth once she'd found out Ryder Trent would be the Kissin' Cowboy. And, who knows, she might even buy a ticket herself. *No, don't go there.* "It's because we'll be, uh…selling tickets for the pleasure—I mean for the chance to, uh…"

Judging from the five-alarm fire that was her face, Ella was pretty sure she probably resembled a ripe tomato. *Great first impression, McIntyre.*

Cassie swatted Ryder on the arm. "Behave and quit teasing her."

"Ouch. What did I do now?" He rubbed his arm in an exaggerated motion. "For someone who wants a favor, you're not being very nice."

Ella watched, fascinated by their sibling exchanges. She'd never had a sibling so she couldn't be sure, but she assumed this was how they acted, even close ones. Somehow witnessing that exchange altered Ella's perception of Ryder Trent. To her, he was more than his reputation as Tenacity's cowboy playboy. Despite his movie-star looks, the way he bantered with his sister, the comfortable slouch of his massive shoulders and the scuff marks on his boots were all signs of a real person, not just the town's heartthrob.

Finding her voice, she gestured toward the back of the library. "Maybe we should take this into the conference room. Shall we?"

"See?" Cassie said, glaring at Ryder. "Your behavior is so bad we've been banished to the back room."

Ryder touched a hand to his chest. "Me?"

"Oh no," Ella practically squeaked and cleared her throat again before continuing, "that's not what I meant. It's just that I set everything up when I came in this morning. I thought we'd be having a…regular meeting."

"Instead you got squabbling siblings," Ryder said with a crooked smile that caused the dimple to peek out again.

"Yes, well…" Ella turned and led the way down the hall. Now the whole idea of a meeting in the conference room sounded pathetic, but she'd started it and intended to finish.

As they walked, she felt the weight of Ryder's presence behind her, like a magnetic field making the small hairs on the back of her neck stand at attention. At least she'd worn her best skirt and blouse today along with her red cowboy boots. They'd been a last-minute choice.

Her boot heels clicked on the library's granite flooring with each step. Damn. The boots might have been a mistake. What had she been thinking? As if she was going to impress Ryder Trent with red boots.

Ryder followed Ella McIntyre down the hall and thanked the library gods for those sexy red boots. And everything else about Ella the librarian. She— *Smack!*

"Hey. What was that for?" he asked in a near whisper.

"I saw that look," Cassie hissed. "And I know what it means."

Before Ryder could respond, Ella had opened the door to the conference room and was waiting for them to enter. The look Ryder shot his sister promised retribution at some future date.

He had to hurry, and all but pushed Cassie out of his way, but he made it in time to pull out Ella's chair with his free hand. *Yeah, you're a real gentleman, Trent.* The thoughts he'd been entertaining about Ella as he followed her down the corridor had been anything but gentlemanly.

Ella seemed surprised by the gesture. "Thank you."

The fact she seemed surprised irritated him, and he wasn't sure why. Could it be, he wondered, that she didn't think he knew how to treat a woman with respect because of his reputation?

Ryder set his hat on the table and pulled out a chair for Cassie before taking one himself. Settling in his seat, his mind went back to Ella's seeming surprise. Could it be because, as Cassie had hinted earlier, Ella didn't date much? If that were the case, what was wrong with the guys in Tenacity? Why weren't they lined up waiting to ask her out?

*Hey, that's a good thing*, he told himself. He wouldn't have to fight a pack of other guys wanting her attention and—

"Isn't that right?"

Cassie's voice interrupted his thoughts.

He glanced at his sister. He'd been zoned out thinking about Ella and her dating life and missed everything else. "Right?"

"I told Ella you're eager to help raise money for the library, even if it means manning a kissing booth."

"When Cassie told me I'd be saving literature for the entire town of Tenacity, I jumped at the chance to help."

"Oh-kay," Ella said and laughed.

He loved the sound of her laugh, throaty and a little husky. Raising his eyebrows, he said, "You don't sound convinced."

"Oh, I don't doubt your sincerity, but I'm not so sure our goal is quite that lofty. Nevertheless, I'm grateful for your help. Thank you."

"You're welcome."

"I must confess I look up to you," Ella told him.

Ignoring Cassie's snicker, he grinned. "That sounds about right. You're what? Five-six? I'm six-two, so it only stands to reason you'd have to look up. Just don't ask me how the atmosphere is up here."

Ella laughed again, her cheeks filling with color. "I promise."

He liked teasing her and getting a reaction. In addition to the color in her cheeks, her light blue eyes sparkled with a combination of affront and amusement. As if she couldn't decide which one she wanted to go with.

A little disconcerting was the fact he'd had no desire to tease any of the women he'd previously dated. Not that he was dating Ella. Did he want to? He glanced at her again. She was beautiful in a girl-next-door way, which was probably why Cassie was shooting him behave-yourself-glares every time he smiled at Ella. Yeah, he wasn't exactly a forever type of guy, and Ella McIntyre looked like a forever type of gal. And yet…

He shifted in the uncomfortable wooden seat. Huh, now it was his turn to have conflicting emotions.

"Actually, I was referring to how you've helped your parents keep the ranch going. I think that's important for the town, too. The people the ranch employs and the goods and services you purchase from local businesses help keep the local economy afloat."

"Thanks, but it's not like the Stargazer Ranch is some big outfit."

"No, but it's still important to Tenacity, and I admire you for staying in town."

Ryder remembered Janelle's criticism of his decision to stay in Tenacity and on the ranch. He looked at Ella more closely. Yep, she sounded sincere, as if she believed what she was saying. Or was she trying to convince herself? Because Janelle had sounded sincere too. Right up until she hadn't.

"I hate to interrupt these special moments, but maybe we should get this meeting started," Cassie said, her gaze bouncing between the two of them.

"Oh…oh…of course," Ella said, looking embarrassed as she picked up a tablet from the conference table. She fumbled with the tablet, nearly dropping it.

"Need help with that?" Ryder reached out, his fingers brushing hers as they both grabbed for the device.

The contact was brief but electric, sending a jolt up Ryder's arm. Ella pulled back as if burned and clutched the tablet to her chest. For the first time in his life, he was jealous of an inanimate object. What was the deal with that? He wasn't some randy teenager anymore.

And yeah, he casually dated a lot of women, but this felt different.

"Ella's been working hard on keeping the library open. I'm hoping we can all help her by pitching in to make this carnival a success," Cassie said.

"Won't you have lots of competition from the annual Valentine dance?" he asked.

"Ours will be on Friday, the day before," Ella said.

Ryder thought for a moment, then raised an eyebrow. "So, we'll be also celebrating Friday the thirteenth?"

"We can't escape the date so we're pretty much stuck with it," Ella said, the color rising in her face.

He liked the way the color accentuated the light dusting of freckles spread across her cheeks. "What else have you got planned for this thing? Besides the kissing booth, that is."

"The Kissin' Cowboy, you mean," Cassie said.

He rolled his eyes at his sister. Ella caught the gesture and laughed, so he winked, causing her to blush again. Damn, since when did he consider that sexy? Probably about the time he decided red cowgirl boots were sexy.

"So, you're going to do it?" Ella asked in a voice that he could only describe as hopeful.

"Of course. Don't let it be said that I was unwilling to help save a pillar of the community from budget cuts."

"I've made a list of possible things we can do and feature, keeping all age groups in mind, along with varying interests." Ella tapped on her tablet and it sprang to life.

"I'm sure Ella and I can handle this from here if you want to pick up Harley now," Cassie said.

"Oh, I wouldn't dream of abandoning you now.

Sounds like this endeavor is going to take a lot of work. Like, all hands on deck." Ryder turned to Ella. "Isn't that right?"

"Uh...well, yes, it will. For some of these ideas to work, we'll need to build a few things. Nothing elaborate, just a few simple booths and displays." She glanced up from her tablet. "Are you good with your hands, by any chance?"

"Well, I—" he began.

Cassie coughed and Ryder threw her a warning look, but all the while he was biting the inside of his cheek. Ella's question was innocent enough, but his thoughts regarding the wholesome librarian weren't. Damn. Was it his turn to blush? If so, he'd never hear the end of it from his sister.

Ella looked up from the tablet and her eyes widened as if just realizing how her question had sounded. She huffed out her breath and slowly shook her head, looking at him and Cassie. "I hate to break it to you, kiddies, but Story Time isn't until tomorrow."

Ella's scolding shocked him, and he hooted with laughter, ignoring his sister's pointed look in his direction. His reaction to her innocent, if poorly worded, question had been juvenile. But more importantly, when was the last time a desirable woman had the power to surprise him?

He was liking Ella the librarian more and more.

Ella groaned inwardly. What must he think of her? Scolding him as if he were a miscreant in one of the various children's activities she conducted. She'd bet none of the other women he'd dated took him to task over a silly, juvenile joke. Not that she ever expected to be one of the women he dated.

But then her gaze collided with his and she ended up laughing, too.

"I guess I should rephrase that. Have you ever done any carpentry work? It's okay if you haven't. I'm sure we can get some other volunteers."

"Let me put it this way—I know my way around a hammer and nails. You need to if you're gonna work on a ranch," he said.

"Of course." Ella nodded. "Fence mending and stuff like that."

Unbidden, her imagination conjured up a vivid picture of a shirtless Ryder Trent mending fences, his muscles rippling with the effort of his work. *Shirtless? Really? Hello. It's February in Montana*, she scolded herself.

"I'll check with Heather and see how she's coming with her list of volunteers and see who on that list is also good at constructing things. I don't think we need anything elaborate," Ella said, pushing away the images her imagination insisted on supplying.

She opened the folder she'd put on the table before the meeting. Pulling out sheets of paper, she said, "I printed out some suggestions I was able to come up with for the carnival and its various components."

She handed printouts to Ryder and Cassie. "We can't do everything, but maybe we can see which ideas would be feasible in the time we have left. I figured I'd write everything down and we could pick and choose."

"I guess there's no way of talking you out of the kissing booth?" Ryder asked.

"Well, I—" Ella began.

"Absolutely not, brother dear," Cassie interrupted. "You're going to be our big moneymaker."

"That's what I'm afraid of," he muttered.

For the next hour and a half, they discussed different ideas and how easy or hard they'd be to accomplish.

Ryder's phone pinged and he pulled it from his front pocket, glancing at the screen with a slight frown. "It's Renee."

Ella watched his fingers fly across the phone screen as he responded to the text. How could just looking at his hands get her all hot and bothered?

"Everything okay?" Cassie asked.

"She's finished with Harley."

"Do German shepherds need grooming?" Ella asked. She knew their sister, Renee, owned a dog-grooming business.

Ryder's left cheek dimpled and she wanted to melt. No wonder all the women in Tenacity, young and old, had a crush on the sexy rancher.

"…cleaning to prevent ear mites," Ryder was saying.

He's speaking, Ella scolded herself. *Quite naming your future children and pay attention.* "I hope he's okay."

"He's fine. Cleaning his ears helps prevent ear mites and Renee's better with things like that," he explained.

"Well, that's good. I think the dog we used to have come for Reading Tails was part German shepherd.

Greta was a sweetheart. The kids really miss her. Too bad her family moved out of the area."

Ryder raised an eyebrow. "You allow dogs to attend Story Time?"

"No, we— Wait, I take that back. I would welcome dogs at the library's Story Time if they were well behaved and housebroken."

"Does that rule apply to the kids, too?" Ryder asked with a twitch of his lips.

Ella chuckled. "*All* children are welcome at Story Time. But Reading Tails isn't a library-sponsored program. It is—*was*—an opportunity for children who struggle with reading to practice. I held it at the community center."

"I understand helping kids with reading, but where does the dog come in?"

"The children read a story to the dog. I had read about therapy dogs helping struggling readers gain confidence. When the community center reached out to me to organize some activities for children, I remembered that and looked into it."

"And it works?" Ryder asked.

"It worked great. The children could read to Greta without fear of judgment, and it worked wonders for their reading skills and confidence."

"Not to mention dogs and children make the perfect combination," Ryder said.

"Exactly." Ella nodded.

"Are you looking for a replacement for Greta?" Cassie asked.

Ella glanced at her friend. She'd almost forgotten

Cassie was in the room, she'd been so focused on Ryder. No wonder so many women had a crush on him. "I have been looking, yes."

"What about Harley?" Cassie glanced at Ryder.

"That's an excellent idea." He nodded. "I can bring him to meet Miss McIntyre tomorrow."

"Oh, I won't be here tomorrow, I'm afraid." She tried to hide her disappointment. "I'll be at the Dinosaur Center and Park. But I'm sure someone at the community center would be happy to meet and evaluate Harley for Reading Tails. I can contact them for you."

Ryder seemed surprised. "I thought the center wasn't even open yet."

"It's not, but we've been lucky with the weather and the construction has proceeded faster than expected. They actually think we'll be able to hold the masquerade ball there next month. I was hired as an education consultant for the center, so I'm helping design and implement education programs and exhibits." Warming to her topic, she continued, "I make sure the exhibits are engaging for all ages and that they're accessible to everyone. Of course, I also have to make sure they align with the center's mission."

"Sounds fascinating. I'd love to hear more," Ryder said.

"You would?" She couldn't help feeling skeptical. She had a tendency to go on about topics that interested her, and most guys tended to tune out.

"Absolutely," he said, that dimple peeking out. "Are you there all day?"

She nodded, feeling tongue-tied again looking at

that dimple. And his voice, that rich baritone, took her breath away.

"But you must get a lunch break. How about if I take you to lunch? We can discuss the carnival and having children read to Harley."

"Well… I…um…"

"Great. It's a date. I'll pick you up at the center. Say, noon?"

"Noon is fine, and I can meet you somewhere if that's easier for you."

He shook his head. "When I ask a woman out, transportation is a given."

Her heart started to beat faster. So maybe this *was* a date?

Ryder held back as Cassie left the conference room and leaned close to Ella's ear. "Be sure to wear those."

Her breath caught in her throat. Ella glanced down at her boots. "O-okay."

With a departing wink, he turned and followed his sister down the hallway.

Still a little stunned, Ella sat as Cassie and Ryder left. She had a lunch date. Wait, was lunch really a date? *It's a date* was just an expression a lot of people used for meetings and such. But he'd said "when I ask a woman out," so that sure sounded like a *date* date. Whatever it was, she'd never been this excited over having lunch.

Because she'd never had lunch with someone as gorgeous and sexy as Ryder Trent. She grinned as she gathered up her tablet and printouts. Maybe the boots hadn't been a bad choice after all.

## *Chapter Three*

Ryder held the heavy wooden door of the Tenacity Public Library open for his sister as they exited to the gabled entry vestibule that projected from the front of the building.

"I can take over from here. You don't have to help plan the carnival," Cassie said as they passed the Tuscan columns flanking the recessed entrance to the historic building.

He blinked against the glare of the February sun and set the Stetson back on his head. "Why are you so concerned?"

"Ella's my friend."

He shook his head as they descended the steps to the sidewalk leading up to the library. "I know she's your friend, but this feels like more."

"I don't know what you mean."

"Knock it off, Cassie. You know exactly what I mean."

She turned to face him. "You don't exactly have a good track record when it comes to single women in this town."

Cassie was right. That thought had been nagging at

him during the meeting, and he didn't need his sister reminding him.

"All we really need is for you to show up for the booth," Cassie said, her tone softer, almost conciliatory.

He didn't want to argue with Cassie, especially when she was right. But all the women he dated knew and accepted that he wasn't going to let himself be roped. He'd tried that once, and the setdown still stung.

"The Kissin' Cowboy, you mean?" He pulled the keys to his battered ranch pickup from his jacket pocket. "Couldn't you come up with a sillier name?"

"I think it's catchy, and Ella seems to like it."

He grumbled but didn't continue the argument. Did Ella really like the idea? Surely she didn't consider him some sort of joke if she'd agreed to have lunch with him. He was taking comfort in that.

"So we're good?" Cassie asked as she opened the passenger door of the truck with a creak of metal.

"Nice try, but I have a date with the librarian tomorrow and I don't intend to break it." He was looking forward to it more than any date he could remember in a long, long time. "You wouldn't want to disappoint her, now would you?"

Cassie glared at him as she settled into the passenger seat. "No. For some unknown reason, she seems to like you."

"There's no accounting for taste," he said as he got into the truck.

The next morning, Ella stood before her closet trying to decide what to wear. This was the first time she'd taken more than five minutes to pull together an outfit for the days she worked at the Tenacity Dinosaur Center and Park. The place wasn't even open to the public yet, so there was no actual dress code. She normally dressed for comfort. But today…

Today was different. Ryder Trent was making it different.

*Face it, Ella, a librarian is hardly his type.*

Nothing would come of it, she told herself as she stared at the meager variety in her closet.

"Looking at your clothes, you'd think you were a square-dancing enthusiast," she muttered, frowning at the denim blouses and flouncy skirts. Ironic, since she couldn't remember the last time she went dancing.

Finally she settled on a billowy white blouse and a calf-length denim skirt. Both would look good with her boots. She still got the tingles when she thought about him whispering his request for her to wear the boots and the sexy wink he'd given her. That purchase had been a rare splurge. One she no longer regretted.

Setting her clothing choices on the bed, she glanced at the antique mahogany highboy dresser that had belonged to her grandmother. She went to stand in front of it, staring at the second drawer.

What would Granny think if she knew what Ella kept in there? She opened the drawer to reveal neat piles of silk and lace. Black. Red. Hot pink. The second drawer of Granny's highboy resembled a Victoria's Secret catalog. Except the drawer—and its contents—were very much *Ella's* secret.

She pulled out a red lace bra. So different from her usual practical choices, it made her smile.

Putting the bra back in the drawer, she decided her everyday plain white cotton was good enough. Besides, a red bra under the white blouse might not be the wisest option. She was working at the center today and wanted to at least give the appearance of being professional. Though she was wearing her hair down instead of in her usual bun.

Ella parked in the as-yet unopened Tenacity Dinosaur Center parking lot. Throwing her winter jacket over her arm, she hurried toward the entrance. Her puffy jacket felt too restrictive when she drove. She'd dithered so much this morning with her wardrobe, she was running a bit late. Not that anyone there was strict about her working hours, but she liked to be punctual.

The construction was still in progress and most of the staff were working in trailers at the site. The three-story cement building that would house the Tenacity Dinosaur Center and Park was nestled in a clearing in the woods with a view of the mountains behind it. Ella slowed her pace to take in the view. It never failed to inspire her.

"Quit dawdling," she told herself and made her way to the trailers outside the building.

As she approached the trailers where they were all working for the time being, Lynda Slater, an attorney who was doing pro bono work for the center, approached her. Lynda was dressed in a conservative gray suit, white blouse and black pumps.

"Good morning, Ella. My, don't you look lovely," Lynda said. "Got a hot date?"

Warmth spread across Ella's cheeks. "Just meeting a…someone for lunch."

"Lucky fella." Lynda tossed her long auburn hair over her shoulder with a big grin. "Love to chat, but I'm running late for another appointment."

Ella nodded and watched Lynda hurry toward the parking lot. Ryder hadn't said where they were going, but it didn't really matter where. Her having lunch with Ryder Trent would be all over Tenacity by this evening.

How did she feel about that? *Conflicted* would be a good place to start.

"Hey, Ella. The meeting is in here," a coworker called from the makeshift break room.

"Coming." Ella grabbed a pencil and pad of paper from her purse.

Technically she wasn't on the planning committee for the masquerade ball, but she sat in on the meetings. As the center's education consultant, she was often asked questions by the committee. The gala event was planned for March, more than a month away.

She frowned. Could she and Cassie pull off *their* event in a much shorter time frame?

And what about Ryder? Would he be a huge help or just a distraction?

Ryder was still asking himself if having lunch with Ella was a good idea when he arrived at the Tenacity Dinosaur Center and Park. The new building would be located not far from where the dinosaur bones had been discovered the previous year. He hoped the center would go a long way toward helping restore Tenacity's finances. He had a stake in this town, for the ranch and for himself. He'd hate for Ella to move away. Whoa! Where'd that thought come from?

He enjoyed meeting and dating women but not once, not since Janelle, had he thought in terms of a future with just one. And he wasn't starting now, he sternly told himself. He'd make sure Ella McIntyre knew that. She was twenty-seven, so it wasn't as if she were some blushing virgin. Although she did blush…

*Just a coincidence*, he told himself.

Feeling better about the situation with Ella and more in control, he parked his truck and made his way to the largest temporary trailer. Once inside the large, open lobby, he spotted several people pouring out of a doorway. It looked as if a meeting of some sort had just adjourned.

His heart rate picked up when he spotted Ella coming toward him, wearing the red cowgirl boots.

"You wore them," he said as she approached, wincing at how breathless he sounded. What was wrong with him? What happened to the pep talk he'd given himself just a few minutes ago?

She gave him a shy grin. "You asked me to wear them."

So that's what happened to the stern talk he'd given himself, he thought as that smile hit him like a punch to the solar plexus.

"Shall we go?" he asked and gave an answering nod to several people who passed him.

"Sure. Let me get my coat and purse," she said and motioned toward a desk and nearby coatrack.

He followed her. "I hope the Silver Spur Café is okay."

"Sounds perfect." She opened the bottom drawer and pulled out a denim drawstring bag with flowers embroidered on it, setting it on top of the desk. She lifted a puffy jacket off the rack. "It's not like there's a whole lot of choice in Tenacity."

He held the jacket for her while she shoved her arms into the sleeves. She zipped it up and freed her hair from under it. His fingers itched to get lost in those strands. Would they be as soft and silky as they looked? He breathed in a whiff of something sweet. He sniffed again.

She glanced at him. "What?"

"Do I smell cake?"

"It's my shampoo. It's called vanilla birthday cake." She picked up the purse and slung it over one shoulder.

"Mmm. I like it," he said as they headed toward the exit.

"Thanks. It's also…"

"Also?" He raised an eyebrow at her.

"It's also a shower gel, or it can be used for a bubble bath," she said in a rush, looking a bit flustered.

"Ooh, I love nothing better than a refreshing bubble bath."

"Yeah, I thought you looked like a bubble bath kinda guy," she responded with a mischievous twitch of her lips.

He fought the urge to reach over and kiss the ghost of a smile off her lips. Getting into a bubble bath with

Ella McIntyre held lots of appeal. Better change the subject before he embarrassed himself. "What I was going to say before we got off topic was that if you'd prefer Mexican for lunch, we can go to Castillo's."

"Not unless you want Mexican." If she was disappointed by the change in topic, she kept it hidden.

"Next time," he said.

She gave him a startled look and stood motionless for a moment. Ah, maybe she wasn't as immune as she first appeared. Good, because he certainly wasn't. He hated to think he might be alone in this…this whatever it was.

"Ready?" he asked, deciding to ignore the fallout from his last comment.

She nodded and fell into step with him as she pulled a pair of gloves from her pocket.

On the way to the restaurant, she told him about the planning meeting regarding the masquerade ball.

"They're all so organized and I feel like we're just throwing this carnival together," she said with a sigh.

"We are."

She turned her head toward him. "That's helpful."

He laughed. "It's not meant to be a formal affair like the ball. People are going to come to this family Valentine's fun, Friday the thirteenth and…"

"Galentine's Day," she supplied.

"Right. Galentine's. They're going to come to this carnival to have some fun and raise money for the library. They won't be expecting perfection."

She gave him a grateful look. "You're right. Thanks for putting it into perspective."

Ryder found a parking spot in front of the Grizzly

Bar, which was located next to the Silver Spur. He hustled out of the truck and around to the passenger side, but Ella already had the door open and was exiting.

"You're supposed to let me do that," he chided.

"Sorry." She blushed. "I guess I'm not used to such gentlemanly treatment."

"Then you've been with the wrong men."

She laughed, but her blue eyes held an expression he couldn't read. Still, his gut reacted to it anyway. Ella might not be the most beautiful woman he'd dated, but there was something about her, a presence, that drew him. Made him want to do things like hold the door open for her. Ella was a woman who deserved to be cherished.

He did hold the door for her as they entered the restaurant. The Silver Spur hummed with activity, as the lunch rush was hitting its peak. The warm, humid air, laden with enticing scents, hit Ryder as he and Ella stepped inside. The din of conversations blended with the soft clinking of silverware and ceramic mugs. Balancing a tray of steaming food, a gray-haired waitress wove her way through the tables and smiled at them.

"Have a seat and I'll be right with you," the waitress said, nodding her head toward a booth near the front windows currently being cleared by a busboy.

Was it his imagination or had some of the conversations paused as he and Ella strolled over to the booth? Several people greeted them, some pretended not to stare and others openly ogled them. He rubbed the back of his neck, minding not so much for himself but for

Ella. She probably didn't appreciate being made the subject of gossip. He was used to it.

"This lunch will not go unnoticed," he told her as they slipped into the booth, facing one another.

"I knew that when I accepted your invitation." She settled her jacket on the bench seat next to her.

And she'd still accepted. The thought made him smile.

"What?" she asked, giving him a quizzical look.

"But you still came with me."

She lifted her chin and glanced around the café. "I did."

Before she could say anything else, the waitress appeared at the table. "Welcome to the Silver Spur. Today's special is chicken and dumplings. Word of advice, whatever you get, be sure to save room for dessert. We have homemade banana cream pie today. It's to die for," she said before scurrying away again.

Ryder glanced around. Many of the patrons were ranchers taking some time out of their schedule, the same as he was. The restaurant served lighter fare, sandwiches and burgers, but always had a hearty special for those hungry ranchers taking a break before returning to more backbreaking work.

The waitress reappeared with red plastic tumblers full of ice water and set them on the table with two straws. "I can come back if you need time to decide."

Ryder glanced at Ella. "Do you need more time?"

She shook her head. "The special sounds good." She smiled at the waitress. "I can't guarantee I'll have room for pie, but I'll do my best."

Ryder ordered the same, and the waitress wove her way back through the scattered tables toward the kitchen.

"So—" Ryder unwrapped the straw "—the library's been through quite a lot these past few years."

He wanted to get to know Ella better and figured talking about the library might be a way to get her to relax a bit. He'd noticed her looking around, aware of the people who kept glancing their way. He hadn't given a lot of thought to his lifestyle until now, but he should have anticipated this.

Ella felt the weight of the other customers' curiosity. Were they wondering why their boring librarian was there with the hottest bachelor in Tenacity?

*Let 'em wonder.* She was going to enjoy every minute of her lunch with Ryder.

"The past couple of years have been a roller coaster ride, that's for sure. Between budget cuts, the constant threat of closure and then all that political drama—" She paused, unwrapping her napkin and setting the silverware next to it. "Tenacity might be small and struggling, but we're colorful."

She was referring to the political scandal involving the former mayor and his wife, who had stolen money from the town's coffers so she could run away with her lover. When it was discovered that money was missing, Mayor Woodson accused an innocent man, knowing full well his wife had stolen the funds. Still, the innocent party was forced to leave town. The true story had finally been exposed, but the shenanigans didn't end there. A new election for mayor ended in a scandal, too.

The waitress returned and set their lunch in front of them, and they continued talking as they ate.

"*Colorful* is the right word. I still can't wrap my head around what happened during the mayor's race," Ryder said, shaking his head. "The whole story about the rigged election is crazy! I'm glad JenniLynn Garrett prevailed in the end. Imagine, her own husband tried to fix it so she wouldn't win. His wife—the mother of his three children." His jaw clenched, and something fierce flashed in those deep blue eyes.

Ella watched as Ryder's strong hands gestured animatedly, his usual lazy drawl picking up speed as he discussed the scandal that had rocked their small Montana town.

"To think someone could do that to their own spouse…" He trailed off, taking a few more hearty bites of chicken and dumplings.

There was a depth to his reaction, something that suggested he held family bonds sacred, despite—or perhaps because of—his reputation as someone who kept emotional distance.

She found herself studying him, noticing how his shoulders tensed as he spoke about family betrayal. It was fascinating to see this side of him—the man behind the flirtatious smirk and devil-may-care attitude that had half the women in Tenacity swooning. For all his reputation as a love-'em-and-leave-'em cowboy, he clearly had strong feelings about family loyalty.

But that shouldn't really surprise her, because his actions proved that. He hadn't left the town and ranching life behind as so many others had.

"It's a horrible story," she agreed, setting her fork down. "Imagine trying to undermine your own spouse like that."

Ryder's laugh was dry, almost bitter. "Which is precisely why I don't understand marriage. People say 'I do' and then everything seems to go downhill from there."

The statement hung between them, loaded with unspoken history. Ella wondered about the experiences that had shaped such a perspective, but she knew better than to press. This was just lunch, not a lifetime commitment, she thought and began eating again.

Ryder leaned back against the red vinyl booth, his expression darkening. "I don't know why people even get married anymore. I certainly have no intention of ever walking down the aisle."

Ella's heart sank just a little, which was ridiculous. Why should Ryder's feelings about matrimony matter to her? They were so obviously a mismatch; the idea of the earnest librarian marrying a roving-eyed cowboy was ludicrous.

She took a sip of water. What was wrong with her? How had this gone from a casual lunch date to the subject of marriage?

She should let it go. She knew she should. But something made her probe further, even as she told herself she was being foolish. "Not all marriages wind up like that, though. Haven't your parents been together a long time?"

Ryder shrugged, his broad shoulders rising and falling beneath his plaid flannel shirt. "Times were different then. People have more options now. Why should anyone settle down?"

Ella lifted her hand, counting off reasons on her fingers. The midday sun streaming through the window caught her nail polish, making it sparkle. "Companionship? Trust?" She ticked off another finger. "Knowing that you'll always have someone who's there for you?"

"Ah, but you can get all that from a dog," Ryder countered, but his eyes crinkled at the corners with amusement. "And I hear they also make good reading companions."

"Can't wait to meet Harley."

"He's really a great dog. Super smart. I'm actually just taking care of him until his owner, Liam Martin, gets back from his tour in the military." He talked about the dog's first encounter with cows and horses and told some other amusing stories about the dog adjusting to ranch life. "At least when Liam gets back, Harley will be used to being on a ranch."

The way his face lit up talking about the dog made something warm flutter in Ella's chest. She laughed, trying to ignore how attractive he looked when he was genuinely excited about something.

"Dogs are great, I'll give you that." She paused, gathering her courage. "But I still hold out hope for the human race. And so, apparently, do your siblings. Your brother and two sisters are all either married or engaged, aren't they? They seem happy."

Something flickered across Ryder's face—uncertainty, maybe, or a shadow of longing he quickly masked. He shrugged again, but this time it seemed more defensive than casual. “Time will tell.”

Ella watched him take a long drink of his water, noting how his throat worked as he swallowed. She shouldn’t find that attractive. She really shouldn’t. But there was something about Ryder that drew her in despite her better judgment. Maybe it was the glimpses of depth she kept catching behind his cavalier facade—the way he spoke about family with such passion, how friendly he was with the waitress, his obvious love for this dog he was temporarily caring for.

The rational part of her brain knew she was setting herself up for disappointment. Ryder had made his views on marriage crystal clear, and she wasn’t the type for casual flings. But her heart wasn’t listening to reason, too busy cataloging the way the sunlight brought out golden highlights in his tousled hair and how his callused fingers wrapped around the red tumbler with surprising grace.

Yeah, she was heading for thin ice and needed to back away. Far away. But as she watched him describe how Harley had appointed himself guardian of the ranch’s chickens, she couldn’t. Nor could she squash the tiny spark of hope that maybe, someday, someone would make Ryder rethink his stance on happily-ever-after. And if her traitorous heart whispered that she wouldn’t mind being that someone? Well, that was between her and her traitorous heart.

# *Chapter Four*

What in the hell was wrong with him? Ryder glanced across the table at Ella, who seemed lost in thought. He didn't blame her after that unleashing of his opinions. Why had he gone on and on about his views on marriage? It wasn't as if someone as smart and serious as Ella McIntyre would hitch her wagon to a rancher with a high school education. According to Cassie, Ella had a master's degree, for crying out loud.

So why had he felt the need to scare her off? And why was he now talking about Harley?

He studied her for a moment, a question forming in his mind. He argued with himself about asking it but finally gave in. "Why are you still here working in a struggling library? With your degree, you could be working in a major city library, doing research, pursuing bigger opportunities."

Ella met his gaze directly. "Tenacity is home."

Her answer had been simple. A statement of fact, nothing remotely apologetic in her tone. There was something profound in those three words—a commitment, a sense of belonging that transcended professional ambition.

But he couldn't help pushing. "Even if the library closes?"

"Even then. But I'm feeling hopeful. Our new mayor seems different. She's got energy, vision. The town needs that right now."

The waitress reappeared to clear away their plates. "So, about that pie…"

Ryder glanced at Ella, who looked torn. "How about we split a piece?"

"Smart man," the waitress said with a grin. "I'll bring a piece with two forks."

After the waitress left, Ella asked, "When can you bring Harley to the community center? I can arrange to have a child there and we can see how a reading session goes."

"You tell me. It may not seem like it, but winter is also a busy time at the ranch, but my schedule is a bit more flexible once the animals are taken care of. I can make repairs on my schedule."

"I can call Heather and see if she can bring Craig in tomorrow. He doesn't really need to practice with his reading, but his mother likes to keep him busy and I owe her."

The waitress brought the pie while they made arrangements and exchanged phone numbers. They took turns eating the pie. He wasn't necessarily big on dessert, but the waitress had been right, it was delicious—and sharing it with Ella made it more special somehow.

He paused with the fork partway to his mouth. Where had that come from? Sure, he enjoyed spending time with women, dating them, getting to know them, but he didn't have sappy thoughts.

Finishing the bite he'd taken, he motioned to the final piece. "You take the last one."

"How about this..." She brought her fork to her mouth with the final piece but only took a small portion. Holding the fork with the remaining bit toward him, she said, "The last bite is always the sweetest."

Against his better judgment, he leaned over the tabletop and closed his mouth around her fork. As he pulled back, he spotted the waitress, who was on her way back to the booth. She broke out in a wide grin. He glanced around and saw others avidly watching and probably itching to relay what they'd seen until everyone in Tenacity, including his meddling family, knew what had happened.

The waitress ripped off a page from her pad and slipped it onto the table with a chuckle. "I see I was right about the pie."

"Sorry about this," he muttered and pulled out his wallet.

Ella shrugged. "No need to apologize. Let's think of this as publicity."

"Publicity?"

"People will be beating down the doors to come to our carnival," she said with a smile.

Ryder tossed enough bills down to cover the meal and a generous tip. He was torn between amusement and irritation. He'd been worried about the gossip and she'd been thinking...what? That this was a publicity stunt?

* * *

Ella regretted her words almost as soon as they left her mouth. But his apology had bugged her. Was he embarrassed that people had seen them together having a moment? From all the gossip she'd heard, he hadn't been *sorry* that other people in Tenacity had seen him dancing, flirting and having a general fun time with the other women he'd dated.

So she'd spouted off that nonsense about this being a publicity stunt. Where that had even come from, she had no idea.

"Ready to go?" he asked.

She nodded and grabbed her jacket. He was probably angry and insulted, and she wouldn't blame him. "I'm sorry. I didn't mean that."

"I'm not sure I follow." He frowned. "Sorry for what? And what didn't you mean?"

"About this being a publicity stunt. I don't think of it as that and I didn't mean to embarrass you."

"Whoa." He put a hand up and leaned closer. He helped her with her jacket. "You did not embarrass me. How would you embarrass me?"

"I'm not exactly the kind of woman you're usually seen with."

"I know."

Her eyes widened. Had she been right all along? "Wh-what?"

He gave her a wicked grin. "You're what those old black-and-white movies call 'a classy dame.'"

She laughed. No one had ever called her a classy dame before. She kinda liked it.

"Let's go before I kiss you and create another scene," he said and took her arm to steer her toward the exit.

Ella's heart fluttered. Kiss her? Oh yes, please. She walked out of the Silver Spur with a big grin on her face as everyone left in the eatery watched them with what could only be described as breathless expectancy.

Oh yeah, everyone in Tenacity would be gossiping about them by tonight, but she found she didn't mind. For once in her life, she wasn't shy Ella McIntyre whom no one barely noticed. The librarian she'd heard a middle school boy call "old lady McIntyre" to one of his friends when she'd admonished his behavior in the library.

Ryder kept hold of her arm as they walked to his car. He probably shouldn't have made that crack about kissing her. But it was true. She'd looked so surprised, and something else, something he wasn't sure of, that he was tempted to lean down and plant one on those lips.

Except he didn't want to rush anything with Ella. What he felt for her was unlike all his other flirtations. She was different. Or maybe he was.

"So is it okay for me to contact Heather and we can set up a time for you to bring Harley to the community center for a Reading Tails session?"

Her question brought him out of his reverie. "Sure. I don't know exactly how long I'll be taking care of him or if Liam Martin will agree to continue the program."

"If you don't want—"

"You're misunderstanding me. I want to do it as long as Harley is agreeable, and I don't see why he wouldn't be. I just want you to understand that it might not be permanent."

They reached his truck, and he opened the passenger door for her, cupping her elbow as she climbed into the seat.

"I understand, but even if it's only temporary, it'll be helpful. Who knows, if word gets out, maybe others will step forward and I can make it permanent."

"Good deal," he said and shut the passenger door.

This reading program was a good thing, but his conscience poked at him, because the biggest reason he wanted to try it was selfish. He wanted to spend more time with Ella.

He watched Ella on her cell phone as he walked around the front of the truck.

"Let me check with Ryder," she was saying as he slipped behind the wheel and shut his door. "She said she can bring Robbie tomorrow around two, if that's okay with you."

"Good with me. What about you?"

She held the phone against her chest as she spoke to him. "It's perfect. I work at the library tomorrow until noon, so I can go over to the community center after and get things set up."

He waited until she'd ended her call then said, "Harley and I can meet you at the library and walk over to the community center with you."

"How about if I provide lunch this time? We can eat at either the library or the community center."

"Sounds like a...plan," he said. He'd almost called it a date again, but something held him back.

"So, do you have any pets?" he asked to break the silence that had descended. Had she noticed his reluctance to call it a date? He couldn't account for that reluctance. "Seems like everyone in Tenacity has at least one dog or cat running around."

Ella sighed. "With three jobs, I barely have time to water my houseplants. Though…"

He glanced at her before concentrating on backing out of the parking spot. "What?"

"I guess I do sort of look after an animal, in a way."

"Yeah?" Ryder eased into an opening in traffic and sped up.

"An opossum started showing up in my backyard last summer. I noticed it was limping a little, so I left out some cut-up apple and sweet potatoes. Now it comes by every night after dark."

Something in her tone made him take a hand off the steering wheel and touch her arm. What sort of reaction had she been expecting? "That's very kind of you. I'm sure finding food during a Montana winter can't be easy for him."

"You don't think it's silly?"

He spared her a quick glance. She sounded surprised by his assertion, which puzzled him. "Why would I think that?"

"Because I'm a grown woman who looks out for a wild marsupial?"

He laughed. "I think it's great that you watch out for the marsupials in Tenacity."

"You probably wouldn't think so if you knew I'd named it, too."

"Oh? What did you name it?"

"Awesome O. Possum."

She sounded embarrassed, so he didn't dare laugh, even if he found it amusing, but not in a denigrating way. "Clever. I like it."

And he liked her. He admired her compassion and he liked that she was sharing things with him, even things she found embarrassing. It was refreshing after the seemingly endless superficial chatter of many of his previous dates. Of course, he'd been the one who'd kept his previous relationships on a superficial level, so he had only himself to blame.

He glanced at Ella and was sorry their lunch had passed so quickly. At least he had tomorrow to look forward to.

Ella gave an inward sigh as Ryder pulled into the same parking spot as before. She had to admit that she was sorry their time together was ending. He, on the other hand, was probably eager to get rid of her. And she wouldn't blame him. She'd spent lunch with the most eligible bachelor in three counties and called it a publicity stunt. As if that weren't bad enough, she'd rambled on about a possum. He probably thought they were a nuisance. If he thought about them at all. No wonder she was perpetually single.

She glanced across the width of the truck cab, but Ryder wasn't looking at her like she was crazy. Instead, his blue eyes had softened with something that looked remarkably like admiration. Was it possible?

"I hope I didn't embarrass you by feeding you that last bite of pie," she said, breaking the silence.

"No way. I think you actually improved my standing in the community."

"I highly doubt that." She huffed out a laugh. "At least I waited until we were alone before going on about the possum."

"That's actually really sweet," he said. "Most people would just ignore an injured animal, especially something like a possum."

"They get such a bad rap," Ella found herself saying, animation creeping back into her voice. "But they're actually beneficial to have around. They eat ticks and other pests, and they almost never carry rabies because their body temperature is too low for the virus to survive. And they're really clean animals, always grooming themselves like cats do. Did you know they're responsible for snake antivenom because they're naturally immune? And that includes rattlesnakes."

She caught herself again and ducked her head. "Sorry, I tend to get carried away with random facts. Hazard of being a librarian, I guess."

"Don't apologize," Ryder said softly. "It's refreshing to meet someone who's so passionate about something, even if it's not what others might consider conventional."

Yeah, that was a good thing to put on a dating profile. *Knows a lot about opossums.*

"Thank you. For everything." She put her hand on the door handle, intent on escaping before embarrassing herself further. "I probably should get back to work."

"Sorry. I hope I didn't make you late."

"No. My hours are flexible as long as I accomplish what I need for the day." She opened the door, then paused. "I guess I'll see you tomorrow."

"Looking forward to it." He tooted his truck horn and waved as he drove off.

*Looking forward to it.* He'd sounded sincere. Was it possible she hadn't scared him off? With his assertion about tomorrow floating around in her head, she went into the trailer with a spring in her step.

The next morning, Ella glanced at her watch as she straightened the books on the display table, adjusting the angle of the latest picture book about farm animals so that it caught the light from the windows. The children's section of the Tenacity Public Library was quiet at the moment. Ninety minutes earlier the place had been abuzz with chatter from three- and four-year-olds enjoying Story Time.

Prior to Story Time, a group of mothers, led by Heather, had approached Ella and offered their help for the carnival. They'd even gotten together and supplied her with a list of tasks they were willing to undertake, including baking treats, face painting, taking pictures and setting up games for youngsters to compete for prizes.

Taking one last look at the area she'd tidied, Ella hurried back to her workstation. Ryder and Harley were due any minute now. Her stomach fluttered at the thought. She tucked a strand of hair behind her ear and glanced at her reflection in the darkened computer screen. Plain. Ordinary. Surely not the type to catch the eye of someone like Ryder Trent, part owner of the sprawling Stargazer Ranch and the subject of constant whispers among the women of Tenacity.

Her description reminded her of her favorite book as a child, *Sarah, Plain and Tall.* She'd overheard one of her visiting aunts talking and calling her plain. At the time, she wasn't sure what it meant, but when she'd spotted the Newbery Medal–winning book, she'd had to have a copy for herself. After reading the book over and over, Ella had decided there was nothing wrong with being plain. And she still felt that way.

Although maybe she didn't need to talk so much about possums. She bet none of the other women Ryder had dated had ever mentioned, let alone listed, the helpful qualities of a wild possum.

"Get it together, Ella," she murmured to herself. "This is about the helping the struggling readers, not you."

What she hadn't counted on was the way her heart raced every time she thought about the tall, broad-shouldered rancher with those piercing blue eyes and that disarming smile.

The sound of the library's front door opening echoed through the quiet space, followed by the controlled click of nails on the granite floor. Ella took a deep breath and smoothed down her navy blue skirt.

"Ella?" Ryder's deep voice carried from the entrance.

"In the children's section," she called back, wincing at the slight tremble in her voice.

And then he was there, filling the doorway with his

presence. Today he wore a crisp white button-down shirt with the sleeves rolled up to reveal tanned forearms, dark jeans and polished boots. His sandy-blond hair was neatly trimmed, but a rebellious lock fell across his forehead. He was also carrying a plastic bag in one hand, but Ella's attention was drawn to his companion. Beside him sat the most dignified German shepherd Ella had ever seen, alert but calm.

"Hey," Ryder said, that slow smile spreading across his face. "Hope we're not late."

"Not at all," Ella managed, forcing herself to meet his gaze. "And you must be Harley," she added, turning her attention back to the dog.

"He is," Ryder confirmed. "I cautioned him to be on his best behavior since we were coming to the library. I remembered what you said about allowing only well-behaved dogs into the building."

His accompanying grin made the hairs on her arms stand up.

He patted the dog's head. "Harley, this is Miss McIntyre."

The dog watched Ella with intelligent eyes, then stepped forward when Ryder gave a subtle hand signal. Harley stopped a respectful distance from Ella and sat, looking up expectantly.

"He's beautiful. Or maybe I should say handsome," Ella said, kneeling to Harley's level.

"Harley, shake."

Ella put out her hand, but instead the dog shook his whole body as if he were wet. She looked expectantly at Ryder, who laughed.

"It's a joke I taught him."

Ella laughed, too, and Harley swiped a paw across his nose.

"I think he's apologizing to you," Ryder said.

Ella reached out and patted the dog's head. "Well, you're forgiven, Harley, but I'm not so sure about your friend here."

The dog chuffed, and Ella looked up at Ryder. "Sounds like he agrees with me."

Ryder laughed. "Don't let him fool you. Now that he's retired, he loves attention."

"Retired?"

"He was an MWD—that's a military working dog to us civilians."

"Impressive." Ella gently stroked Harley's head, marveling at how soft his fur was. The dog leaned into her touch slightly, and Ella felt her tension begin to melt away.

"You're a natural with him," Ryder observed, his voice softening. "Some people can be a little intimidated at first."

"I love dogs," Ella confessed, standing back up.

"And possums," Ryder added with a chuckle.

Harley whined.

"I told him about your possum and now he can't wait to meet him," Ryder said.

"I'm sure Harley is a good boy, but I'm not sure the possum would feel the same."

Harley tipped his head to the side as if following the conversation, and Ryder chuckled. "You're probably right."

"But he's welcome to observe Awesome through the window of the patio door, the same way I do."

Ryder raised an eyebrow. "Oh."

Was she really going to do this? She inhaled. "You're invited, too. If the two of you would like to come over for supper some night."

"Considering Harley doesn't drive, I'd be happy to accompany him. When's a good night for you?"

"Tomorrow?" Yeah, that was real subtle. *He'll probably—*

"We'd love to. Wouldn't we, Harley?" Ryder said, and Harley gave a short bark and wagged his tail.

"Okay. Good." There was an awkward moment as they stared at one another.

Harley broke the tension with a short bark.

Ryder looked sheepish and handed Ella the bag. "I almost forgot. I ran some errands this morning and picked these up. I thought they might be good for the reading thing. That is, if you think they're okay."

Ella opened the bag. It contained several children's books.

"You didn't have to do—" she began as she pulled out the books. They were all stories involving opossums. "Oh my."

"Are they okay?" he asked, stepping closer. "I don't know much about picking out children's books."

She leaned forward as she answered, "They're perfect."

"I figured the kids might want to keep one after they've read it. If all goes well."

Warmth spread through her chest at his hopeful tone.

"That's very generous of you. I'm sure the children will be thrilled. Maybe this will turn them into lifelong readers."

"And future library patrons?"

"Are you accusing me of being self-serving?"

"Ella, you are one of the most generous, compassionate women I know."

"Gee, thanks." She clutched the books to her chest and did her best to smile at the compliment. And it most definitely was a compliment. Just not what she'd been hoping for from the sexy cowboy of her dreams last night. There was nothing wrong with generous and compassionate. But what about passionate or sexy or anything along those lines? This was equivalent to *she has a great personality* when asked if she was pretty.

Would he have said that if she'd been wearing something from her secret pleasures drawer? Of course, even if she had, he wouldn't know it unless she threw off her clothes. In front of him. In the public library. In the children's section.

*Get a grip, Ella.*

# *Chapter Five*

Ryder shifted his weight from one foot to the other. Judging by the emotions crossing her face, he'd just walked into a pasture littered with cow pies without watching where he was stepping.

*Smooth move, Trent.*

Harley made a grumbling sound in his throat, making Ryder glance down at him. Even the dog knew he'd taken a wrong step.

"Did I say something wrong? I meant it as a compliment," he said, wincing at how defensive he sounded.

"I *know* it was a compliment, and I thanked you," she said, but still sounded testy.

"Then I'm not sure what the problem is." He rubbed a hand across his chin.

"There isn't one."

Needing to get the air cleared, he twirled an index finger in a circle. "See, now that's where we disagree."

Why didn't he just take her at face value and drop this? With any other woman, he would have but not Ella. He wanted the air cleared between them. He wanted—*Oh God!*

"I basically called you nice, and while there's nothing wrong with that… I have two sisters. That is not what a gal wants to hear from a guy." *Especially one they like*, he added silently. Maybe he was learning to avoid those cow pies.

"Cassie and Renee taught you well. On the outside I might be a mild-mannered librarian, but underneath this outfit could be…"

"Could be what? Red lace?" he prompted. Yeah, like he needed more fuel for his imagination when it came to Ella. Why had he thrown that out there?

Judging by the color in her cheeks, he might be right and silently groaned. He—

Harley broke the tension with a short, sharp bark.

They both laughed and she said, "I think he's eager to get started with his new duties."

"I think you're right." He scratched the dog behind his ears and thanked him for the interruption.

Except now he'd be wondering what Ella had on beneath those librarian outfits. Most of the other women he'd dated hadn't been shy about advertising their assets to attract his attention. But Ella was different and that in and of itself was enough to make him uneasy.

And she never did answer the question about the sexy underwear, so he was left to his own devices.

Who knew his imagination could be so vivid?

After eating the sandwiches, potato chips and cookies Ella had brought with her, they walked over to the community center. The air was crisp but the sun was shining, so it made for a pleasant walk.

As they walked, Ella tried not to notice the way the

sunlight caught in Ryder's hair or how his eyes crinkled at the corners when he smiled. *Professionalism*, she reminded herself. Today was supposed to be about the children's reading program, not her ridiculous crush on a man who saw her as generous and compassionate. He was helping her with this and with the fundraising carnival, not romancing her. She needed to remember that.

"Harley appreciated the dog biscuits you brought for him," Ryder said as they followed the sidewalk to their destination.

"Well, he's certainly welcome. I appreciate his willingness to help with the kids," she told him.

Once inside the building that housed the Tenacity Community Center, Ella led Ryder and Harley into one of the rooms.

"I've set up a special corner for the reading sessions," she said, gesturing to an area with a large round rug surrounded by bookshelves. "I thought we could start with introducing Harley to Craig and his mom. Maybe you could explain a little about German shepherds. Knowing Craig, he'll have a ton of questions about Harley and even about ranch life. Would that be okay? I found some books you could show him about German shepherds and ranch life."

"Sure."

"I...um... I didn't realize you'd be bringing some possum books, which I love, and I hope some of the kids will want to read them in the future. If this gets off the ground."

"It will."

"You sound pretty confident."

"I am. My sister Renee said she's going to ask some dog owners if they'd be interested. She gets to know dogs in her grooming business, so she'd know which ones were the best suited."

"That's wonderful. Thank you. And thank you for bringing books for them to keep. I'm sure they'll be thrilled. Some of these kids' families struggle and books are a luxury. That's why the library is so important."

Ryder took the books, his fingers brushing against hers. Ella felt a spark of electricity at the contact and quickly pulled her hand away.

"I hope I won't be putting you out of job by giving them books to keep." His eyes were crinkled in the corners.

"Bring it on, cowboy," she joked and was rewarded when he chuckled.

"How often were you thinking of running this?"

"I was hoping for once a week," Ella said. "But I understand if that's too much of a commitment with the ranch and everything." She was suddenly aware that she might be asking too much of a man who surely had better things to do than spend time bringing his temporary dog to the community center.

To her surprise, Ryder's face lit up. "Once a week sounds good. Tuesdays work best for me, if that fits your schedule. Things tend to be quieter at the ranch then."

"Tuesdays would be perfect," she said, unable to hide her smile. "I only work mornings at the library and we'll need to wait for school to be out."

"Could you approach the school about holding the

sessions there? If we can do some of it during school hours, we can fit in more kids."

"That's a great idea. You'd be okay with that?"

"Absolutely," Ryder said, holding her gaze a moment longer than necessary. "Harley and I are at your service."

Harley gave a soft woof as if in agreement.

"He approves," Ryder chuckled.

"I'm glad to hear it. Would you like to see where you'll be sitting? I've arranged some comfortable pillows for Harley."

"Don't worry about Harley. Since he was in the military, I doubt he had many luxuries when he and Liam were on patrol."

Harley whined, and Ella knelt down in front of the dog and gently took his head in both her hands and said, "And we appreciate your service, soldier."

She started to rise, and Ryder reached down to help her up. He held her hand and looked at her, his gaze coming to rest on her lips. Her heart began to beat erratically and her tongue swiped across her bottom lip. Ryder's eyes darkened at the gesture and he began to lean closer and—

A door slammed followed by a woman's chastising voice. "Craig, don't run."

Ella and Ryder jumped apart. Ella spared Ryder a final glance. Was that regret on his face? If so, hers probably reflected the same sentiment.

Forty-five minutes later, Ryder held the door for her as they left the community center and stepped out into the afternoon sunshine. His hand found the small of her back, just for a moment, but it was enough to send a shiver down her spine even through her puffy jacket.

"I think that went well," Ryder said.

"It did. I can't thank you enough, and Harley, too, of course." Ella patted Harley on the head. "And that was kind of you to let Craig have one of the possum books."

"My pleasure. I'm looking forward to the meeting," Ryder replied with a teasing smile. "Though I hear they're not big on formal introductions."

She rolled her eyes, but an idea occurred to her and she was speaking before she'd thought it through. "Well, I can't guarantee a meeting but Awesome usually shows up while I'm cleaning up after supper."

"We're both looking forward to it."

She was encouraged by his quick response. "So am I."

"What can I bring? I know how busy you are and I don't want to impose on your hospitality."

"Not an imposition. I can throw something in the slow cooker tomorrow morning before I leave for work. It's nice to cook for more than just myself." She was already thinking about what she had on hand that she could throw together.

"If you're sure..."

Oh, she was sure. "Do you like chicken cacciatore? It's quick, easy and delicious in the slow cooker."

"Sounds great. How about if I stop at Tenacity Grocery and pick up some garlic bread? If you think that would go with it."

"Perfect, and that way I can go straight home from

work." Ella's footsteps slowed as they neared the library. She was sorry to see their time together come to an end, but she had tomorrow night to look forward to.

Ryder glanced at the library. "I never thought much about the library before. Even the building itself is impressive."

"It's beautiful but eats money."

"Hopefully our carnival will help with that. I hate to think your job might be in jeopardy. You're so dedicated."

Ella shrugged. "I love what I do."

"It shows," Ryder said. "Your face lights up when you talk about books and reading programs."

Ella felt heat rise to her cheeks. "Books have always been my escape," she admitted. "Other worlds to explore without ever leaving home."

"I've always found my escape on horseback," Ryder said. "Something about the open land, the connection with the animal beneath you." He paused, then added, "Maybe we should trade sometime. You teach me about your world, I'll teach you about mine."

"I'd love that." She wasn't going to admit the thought of riding a horse intimidated her, but she'd get over it if it meant spending more time with Ryder.

"Have you never ridden?" He sounded surprised and continued when she shook her head. "How did that happen? You've lived in Tenacity all your life, haven't you?"

"It's my shameful secret."

He laughed and tweaked her nose. "Well, I intend to do something about that, Ella McIntyre."

Ella watched him and Harley get into his truck, waving as they drove off. She slowly pulled her keys out of her purse and got into her aging Toyota.

*I intend to do something about that, Ella McIntyre.*

His words echoed in her head all the way home. He'd been referring to her never having ridden a horse, but her imagination kept supplying other scenarios to his words.

*Get real*, she told herself as she pulled into the driveway of the modest two-story home that her great-grandfather had built with a kit ordered from the Sears catalog. Her parents had made upgrades to it, and when they'd moved away from Tenacity, she'd bought it from them. She'd had plans to do more updates, but Tenacity had fallen on hard times and money was tight. *Someday*, she'd told herself.

Just as she'd told herself she'd someday meet someone who appreciated her. Was that man Ryder Trent, or was she writing checks she couldn't cash?

The next morning Ryder was alone in the kitchen of the home he shared with his parents and Cassie on the Stargazer Ranch. Enjoying a second cup of coffee before beginning his chores, he stood at the sink and stared out of the window above it.

"Glad you're still here," Cassie said as she entered the spacious kitchen. "I was hoping to catch you before you left."

He set the empty mug in the sink and turned around. "You're an early riser today. What's up?"

"I heard you're having dinner at Ella's tonight."

A smile touched his lips. "News travels fast in small towns."

"Actually, Mom told me. You told her you wouldn't be here for family dinner."

"Graham can take my place at the table."

"Listen, Ryder." Cassie crossed her arms. "Ella's… different."

*I don't need you to tell me that.* But he figured his sister wasn't thinking in the same terms as he was about Ella McIntyre. "What do you mean by that?"

Cassie opened her mouth, then closed it again, clearly wrestling with something. "She's just…serious. About everything she does. Including relationships."

Ryder studied his sister's face, sensing there was more she wasn't saying. "And?"

"Just…don't mess around with her, okay? She's not like the other women you've dated."

"Who says we're dating? We're working on planning the carnival and getting Harley ready for her Reading Tails project."

While this was true in a strict sense, Ryder wanted more from his interactions with Ella, but he wasn't about to admit that to his meddling sister.

Cassie's eyes narrowed. "You're sure that's all?"

"Look, Cassie, I can appreciate your concern, but Ella is an adult. If she wants to invite Harley and me to supper, she's allowed to without interference from you. No matter how well-intentioned that meddling might be."

She sighed. "You're right."

"Look, I've got to get going. I need to check those fences in the north pasture."

As he walked away, Cassie's words echoed in his mind. The warning should have made him want to back off, to keep things purely professional. Instead, he found himself thinking about the way Ella's eyes sparkled when she laughed, how she'd spent time explaining the history of the library's architecture to him, her face animated with enthusiasm. Yes, she was serious about her work and her studies, but he'd also seen her stringing fairy lights in the community center's reading nook, humming Disney songs under her breath. He'd watched her get into a passionate debate about the differences between manga and comic books with a teenager at the center and later offer to help him set up a manga readers' group at the library.

Running a hand through his hair, Ryder realized he was in dangerous territory. For the first time in his life, he was the one who needed to be careful. He couldn't remember ever feeling this way about a woman before—this mixture of attraction, admiration and something deeper he wasn't ready to name. Ella wasn't just beautiful; she was brilliant, kind and unexpectedly funny. The way she bit her lower lip when she was concentrating, how her eyes lit up when she talked about books, the slight tremor in her hands when their fingers brushed as she handed him a possum book yesterday—all of it was driving him crazy.

Maybe Cassie was right to warn him off. But as he pictured Ella in her library, surrounded by her beloved books, Ryder wondered if it was already too late. The question wasn't whether he should pursue her anymore, but whether he was worthy of someone like Ella—someone who approached love with the same dedication and sincerity she brought to everything else in her life.

As he headed to the barn to saddle his horse, Ryder found himself planning what to wear to dinner, wondering if he should stop for wine and hoping Ella would wear her hair down the way she had yesterday. He was in trouble, all right. And for once in his life, he didn't mind at all.

Ella sat at the reference desk that afternoon, surrounded by a scatter of papers and wearing her reading glasses. Her librarian glasses, as she thought of them. The sun glinted through the nearby window, casting long shadows across the polished wooden floors. Ella breathed in the familiar scents of books and lemon polish, but no matter how much she tried to concentrate on the paperwork in front of her, her mind kept taking detours. And a certain tall, muscly cowboy was to blame.

"Hard at work?"

Ella's head popped up at the sound of her friend's voice. "Hardly working is more like it."

"Ready for another fundraiser meeting?" Cassie asked, leaning against the desk. "I noticed some of the other volunteers heading to the conference room."

Ella's face lit up, and she pushed her glasses higher on her nose. "Oh my gosh, I totally lost track of the time."

She shuffled through some papers, pulling out a detailed spreadsheet. "And Ryder has been absolutely amazing. He's been emailing me whenever he gets a new idea."

Cassie's eyebrows rose at the mention of Ryder's name. "He's certainly gotten involved beyond the kissing booth, hasn't he?"

"Actually, he and Harley are coming over for supper tonight. I'm making that chicken cacciatore slow cooker recipe that you gave me." Ella's cheeks flushed slightly as she spoke.

"Ella, you know his reputation around town. He's dated half the women in Tenacity." Cassie's voice sharpened slightly. "And the other half are either married, involved, related to us or too young."

Ella laughed, seeming to wave away Cassie's concern. But she'd had some of the same thoughts. "You worry too much. We're just friends working on the fundraiser and a reading project."

"I heard he's helping with Reading Tails."

"News travels fast. And Harley is the one being read to."

"I just…" Cassie lowered her voice, glancing around the quiet library. "You haven't had as much experience as my brother has in the romance department. I don't want to see you get hurt."

Why did people seem to think she couldn't take care of herself? Did she give off helpless vibes?

"I appreciate your concern. I really do, but I'm an adult," Ella pointed out.

"Yeah, that's what—"

"That's what what?"

"Oh, nothing. It's just that I realized I shouldn't be meddling," Cassie said airily.

Ella didn't quite believe her, but one of the mothers came looking for her for the planning meeting. She managed to keep her mind on the subject at hand for the rest of the afternoon. But in the back of her mind, Ryder still lurked.

Ryder glanced at Ella's house through his windshield. The 1920s-era Sears catalog home stood proudly against the February twilight, its welcoming front porch illuminated by a string of soft yellow lights. Ryder had looked up her home, and despite the passage of time—nearly a century—many of the original features of the Fullerton remained. Most notable were the flared columns on the front porch with the paneled columns on top. The Fullerton's three windows on the home's front, and the small "landing window" on the side remained intact. Above the porch was the attic's broad, low dormer window with an undersized sash. The modest structure had a dignified air that somehow matched its owner perfectly. Like Ella, the house was unpretentious yet possessed a quiet elegance that caught you by surprise once you got to know her.

Harley looked at him from the passenger seat, tilted his head and whined.

"Yeah, I know, but for some reason Ella gives me sappy thoughts." He gently took the dog's head between his palms and rubbed. "But that's our secret, okay?"

The dog woofed in agreement as Ryder reached into the back seat to retrieve the bag he'd brought.

The Montana winter air bit at his cheeks as he and Harley made their way up the shoveled path. Had Ella shoveled that herself? Maybe he could help next time. Yeah right, like he had time for that along with his ranch chores. Maybe he could arrange for someone like a teenage neighbor to do it. Liking that solution, he bounded up the steps to her porch.

The open porch was decorated with two sturdy wooden rockers, and he pictured the two of them seated there on a warm summer night. He shook his head at the picture. What was getting into him?

The dog sat on his haunches and tilted his head at Ryder.

"Again, our secret," Ryder reminded him with a finger to his lips.

He'd traded his usual battered Stetson for a newer one, and instead of his work-stained ranch clothes, he wore his best dark jeans and a pressed button-down shirt under his shearling jacket. The cologne he'd dashed on—a Christmas gift from his sister Renee that he'd never opened until tonight—felt like a confession of something he wasn't ready to admit.

Before he could knock, the door swung open. Ella stood there, her usual librarian bun replaced by loose blond waves that framed her face. She wore a simple orange sweaterdress that hugged curves usually hidden beneath cardigans and practical skirts.

"You planning to stand out there all night?" Her smile reached her eyes, crinkling the corners. "It's twenty degrees and dropping. Poor Harley isn't as warmly dressed as you."

She bent at the waist and gave the dog a warm welcome.

"Just admiring the architecture," Ryder fibbed smoothly, stepping into the warmth of her home, followed closely by Harley. The scents of tomatoes, peppers and garlic wrapped around him like a welcome. "This is a genuine Sears Fullerton home, right? My grandmother had catalogs from that era. Used to flip through them when I was a kid."

"It is a Fullerton. I'm impressed," Ella said, taking his jacket. Her fingers brushed his shoulders, and he fought the ridiculous urge to lean into her touch. "My great-grandparents ordered it in 1929, right before the crash. Family legend says they had to scrimp and save for years before and after, but they never regretted it."

"It's perfect," Ryder said, meaning it. "Very you."

"Thank you, I think." A blush touched her cheeks. "Would you two like a tour before dinner?"

"Lead the way."

He and Harley followed her through the roughly nineteen hundred square feet of thoughtfully arranged space. The living room welcomed them first with a brick fireplace where flames danced behind a glass door. Original oak flooring gleamed beneath their feet, the patina of nearly a century of footsteps giving it a warm, honeyed glow.

"Love these creaky old floors," he said.

She chuckled. "Yeah, there was never any sneaking home after curfew when I was growing up."

"I can't imagine you breaking curfew."

"You'd be surprised," she responded with a glint in her eyes.

He leaned closer. "Do tell, Miss McIntyre."

Harley pushed between them and woofed.

Ryder shook his head. "And who appointed you chaperone?"

Ella laughed but continued the tour of her home. Ryder silently told the dog he would deal with him later. Harley followed them as they trooped up the stairs. Evidently the dog had appointed himself guardian of Ella's virtue. Had Cassie had a talk with the dog without his knowledge?

Ryder took in her bedroom from the doorway. Feminine without being fussy. The neatly made bed made him ashamed of the jumble of covers on his. Of course, if Ella ever came to the ranch house, he'd be sure to rectify that.

"This is where I spend most of my evenings," Ella said once they were back downstairs, gesturing to a well-loved armchair positioned by the fireplace. A small table beside it held a stack of books, a half-empty teacup and reading glasses perched atop a dog-eared paperback.

"Let me guess," Ryder said, leaning to read the spine. "Jane Austen?"

"Good eye, cowboy," she smiled. "*Pride and Prejudice.* My comfort read."

"Darcy's a bit stiff for my taste."

Ella raised an eyebrow. "You've read Austen?"

"I read everything. Ranching involves more downtime than people might think. Especially winter nights." He shrugged, enjoying her surprise. His dysgraphia hadn't prevented him from reading—it wasn't like dyslexia. No, it just prevented him from writing a coherent report on what he'd read. That's why educators had, among other things, labeled him lazy or uncaring. If he could read, why couldn't he write a book report or a term paper?

He blocked those thoughts as they moved to the formal dining room, where she'd set a table with what appeared to be heirloom china, delicate blue flowers circling white plates. A built-in cabinet displayed more matching pieces.

"My grandmother's," she explained, noticing his gaze. "Only comes out for special occasions."

The implication hung between them. This was a special occasion.

## *Chapter Six*

Ella pointed to the bag Ryder had set on the couch before taking a tour of her house. Pleased that he'd been interested in the history of her home, she'd forgotten to ask him about it so was doing so now. "Is that the garlic bread?"

He picked up the bag. "Yes, and also something for your little friend."

"My friend?"

"Awesome?" Ryder pulled a bunch of grapes from the bag. "I know you said you feed him apples and sweet potatoes so I looked up to see what else it might like. I gather grapes are a favored treat. I didn't want to bring anything inappropriate."

The simple thoughtfulness of the gesture made her heart squeeze. Here was this man—this gorgeous, capable man who could probably have any woman in three counties—researching possum diets because he'd wanted to be sure what he brought was safe.

"That's so sweet of you," she managed, taking the grapes and potato and setting them on her entry table. "Though I should warn you, he's not the most sociable creature. Mostly shows up for his snacks and disappears if I try to say hello. So I just watch respectfully through the window."

"Sounds like our old barn cat, Calico." Ryder's chuckle was warm honey in the air between them. "We had her for over fifteen years and she'd always have this *do I know you* look if food wasn't involved."

"I didn't have any pets growing up. My father was allergic." She sighed. "And now I'm not home enough. It wouldn't be fair."

They ended the tour of her three-bedroom home in the kitchen, where Ella busied herself with final dinner preparations. Ryder got Harley settled with a water bowl. The domesticity of it all made her chest ache. It was too easy to imagine this as their routine—sharing meals, caring for their pets, moving around each other with comfortable familiarity.

But she needed to be careful. She hadn't known him long but had noticed Ryder was naturally kind to everyone. His thoughtfulness wasn't special treatment, just his way of moving through the world. She couldn't mistake friendship for something more just because she longed for it to be.

Or, if it was more, that it would last. What made her think she'd be the one to convince the perennial playboy to settle down? This wasn't one of the romance novels she checked out of the library.

Ryder enjoyed watching Ella putter around her kitchen. Normally, thoughts of domesticity caused him to break out in a sweat or made him want to run the other way. Strangely, he wasn't feeling the least bit hemmed in. At least not tonight in Ella's kitchen. Maybe in the light of day tomorrow he'd feel differently. For tonight, though, he was intoxicated by Ella and the smell of tomatoes and herbs.

Over chicken cacciatore with pasta and garlic bread, they batted around ideas for the fundraising carnival, with Ella taking notes.

Harley had been quiet and unobtrusive during dinner but got up and gave him the dog equivalent of puppy eyes when Ella brought out her brownies and ice cream.

"Sorry, but chocolate is a no-no for dogs," Ryder told him.

"It's okay, Harley. While Ryder was getting treats for the possum, I was thinking of you," Ella told him and went to the freezer. Removing a small container, she said, "I believe this is the equivalent of ice cream for dogs. It's made for them, so I assume it's safe."

She gave a sudden frown and turned to Ryder. "Oops, maybe I should have checked with you first."

Ryder nodded and watched as Ella set the treat down for an eager Harley. "That's very sweet of you. Thank you. You've made this night special."

She blushed and said, "You've made it special for me. I can't remember the last time I had company to cook for."

"You don't have relatives in town?"

"No. My parents moved to Florida several years ago after my grandma died. They couldn't wait to leave and wanted me to come, but Tenacity is home."

"You don't mind the harsh winters?"

"No. You know what they say—if you're cold then you're wearing the wrong clothes."

Ryder chuckled and agreed.

After they'd cleaned up the kitchen, Ella got out an apple and a sweet potato. Cutting each in half, she said, "I'll cut the halves into smaller pieces, then save the rest for tomorrow."

She cut the apple and potato into bite-size pieces and put them on a plate with the grapes, which she'd also halved. After putting out the plate of food and leaving her back light on, Ella made coffee and they sat at the kitchen table instead of in the dining room. They discussed some more ideas about the carnival until Harley got up from his spot on the floor and went to the back door and whined.

"Either he wants to go out or your friend is here," Ryder said.

They got up and went to the window near the back door. Sure enough, a possum was busy eating the treats Ella had set out. Ryder hadn't thought much about the elusive creatures until now. He had to admit it might not be the most attractive animal, but it held a certain appeal. This one had gray outer hairs over the much lighter hairs underneath, giving it a frosted appearance. The fur on its face was white, and it had a pink nose with white whiskers and black ears.

"How do you know it's the same one each night?" Ryder asked as he watched it enjoy the grapes he'd brought.

"I've had others a few times, but Awesome has a very dark gray patch on his back. Or maybe her back. I honestly don't know."

Ryder nodded. "Okay, I see the patch. It's almost like a black square."

Harley whined again and pawed at the door.

"Do you think he needs to go out?" Ella asked.

"I think he knows Awesome is there and wants to introduce himself," Ryder said. "But I could be wrong. Would you be interested in a walk? We could go out the front door and walk down the sidewalk. You said the cold didn't bother you."

"That sounds like a challenge."

He grinned when she lifted her chin as if rising to the challenge. "Well…"

"You're on. The sky is supposed to be pretty clear tonight, so maybe we can spot some stars."

"Do you enjoy stargazing?" Ryder asked as an idea occurred to him.

"I do. I may not know their names, but I like looking at them."

He did his best to look appalled. "I would have thought you'd know all the names and where they were in the sky."

"I'll be sure to put astronomy books on my list of reading material," she said with a laugh.

"There's some spots on the ranch that are very good for viewing. After all, it's called the Stargazer Ranch," he said with a chuckle. "Of course, the prime spots are a bit remote, not easy to get to in the winter. Have you ever used snowshoes?"

"Snowshoes? No, never, but they look like fun."

"I'm not sure fun is the first thing that comes to mind, but how about a lesson? And, if you'd like, I can check the University of Alaska aurora forecast site.

Can't guarantee we'll see anything, but it can't hurt to plan around that."

Her face lit up. "Oh, do you think we could? I would love that, even if we only see stars."

"Sure. I'll get some information and we can make plans."

Harley gave a short, sharp bark.

Ryder laughed and patted the dog. "We haven't forgotten we promised you a walk, buddy."

"Let me get my coat, hat and mittens," Ella said. "As I said, I don't mind the cold, but I do respect it."

"Good call." Ryder glanced out the window. "Your possum finished his snack and left."

"Then maybe Harley does need to go out," Ella said as she put on her jacket followed by hat and mittens. "Damn, forgot my scarf," she said and started to pull off her mittens.

"Wait. Let me," he said and reached over to grab her scarf off the table where she'd laid it.

His gaze met and held hers as he partially unzipped her jacket. He tucked the scarf under the jacket and around her neck. Slowly his hands reached up and adjusted her scarf before zipping up her jacket.

Ella swallowed, and Ryder caught the movement. It sparked something in his belly.

He stepped back before the simple act turned into something else.

It wasn't easy, but Ella did her best to dismiss Ryder's simple act of helping with her scarf.

*Enjoy what's happening now and let the future take care of itself,* she warned herself.

The night was crisp and stars were scattered across the velvet sky like diamond dust. Ella huddled into her jacket as they set off down her quiet street, Harley's leash swinging between them.

"Where are you working tomorrow? Library or Dinosaur Center?" Ryder asked, his boots striking a steady rhythm on the pavement.

"I was supposed to work at the library all day, but Millie has given me the afternoon off to go to the city to get some craft supplies for the carnival. The volunteer mothers want to set up a spot to make friendship bracelets. We thought it would be a good Galentine's Day craft."

"Perfect timing," Ryder said with a smile.

Ella couldn't see him clearly in the light from the moon, but she imagined his eyes crinkling in the corners. "What do you mean?"

"Harley's got a hospital appointment tomorrow in the city," Ryder said as they rounded a corner.

Ella's heart dropped. There was a specialized veterinary hospital in Bronco. "Is everything okay? He seems fine, but—"

"Oh!" Ryder interrupted her. "No, sorry, not that kind of appointment. We're headed to Bronco Valley Hospital. The pediatric ward."

"The pediatric ward?" Ella glanced down at Harley, who was trotting along contentedly.

"My sister Renee got special permission for him to visit the children," Ryder explained. "The son of a friend of hers is getting treatment."

"That's wonderful," she said softly, meaning it with every fiber of her being. Tenacity's playboy wasn't anything like she'd imagined. He was a man who brought grapes for possums and spent his time bringing a dog to visit sick children. Ella wasn't sure her heart could take much more.

"Yeah, my sisters love to volunteer me for things."

"It's still a wonderful thing to do." She thought about pointing out that, while they might volunteer him, he always agreed to do it, but she decided to keep that to herself.

Ryder was quiet for a moment, and she could feel him gathering his thoughts. When he spoke again, his voice held a note of uncertainty she'd never heard before. "I was thinking…since you're planning to go anyway… maybe you'd like to come with us?"

Ella's step faltered, and she looked up. His face was in shadow, but his voice had held a note of vulnerability. This wasn't just a casual invitation—she could feel the weight of meaning behind it, the way it felt like more than just a hospital visit.

"I'd love to," she said, her voice barely above a whisper.

His smile bloomed slow and sweet in the moonlight. "I can drop by the library and pick you up. Or did you want to go home first?"

"The library is fine," she said.

Maybe she wasn't the only one feeling like this could be something more. Maybe, just maybe, she wasn't alone in wanting their story to be more than working on a carnival together. Something that would end on Valentine's eve.

Above them, a shooting star traced a bright path across the night sky, and Ella made a wish she didn't dare say aloud. Some wishes had a way of coming true all on their own.

The sharp cold of a February breeze bit at Ryder's face as he leaned against his weathered pickup in front of the Tenacity Public Library. His gloved hands were shoved deep in the pockets of his sheepskin jacket, a habit from years of Montana winters.

He was still arguing with himself over last night. Should he have kissed Ella before he left? He'd wanted to but then chickened out at the last minute. What if she didn't feel that way about him? Would she pity him if she realized how he felt but didn't return that attraction?

He'd had enough pity to last him a lifetime. Family and teachers had pitied him during his struggles in school. By the time they diagnosed his dysgraphia, he'd soured on school and decided against college. He'd decided to stay in Tenacity and work the ranch. An honest living carrying on a tradition and making sure his family's legacy, Stargazer Ranch, survived. His ex Janelle hadn't seen it that way. She'd said she pitied him for his inability to make something of himself.

Without conscious thought, he'd curled his hands into fists but as soon as he spotted Ella coming out of the library's front door, his hands unclenched.

He straightened up from his slouch, watching as Ella turned to shut the door. Even from this distance, the sight of her caused a familiar tightness in his chest. Her burgundy coat hugged her slender frame, and she'd wrapped her cream-colored scarf around her neck. Her face lit up with a smile that warmed him despite the frigid air.

"You're early. You should have come inside," she called, her voice carrying in the crisp air as she practically skipped down the sidewalk toward him.

"I didn't want to leave Harley in the cold."

Ella reached him, her cheeks already flushed from the chill, eyes bright. "I told you he's welcome any time."

"We weren't here long," he said, opening the passenger door and ordering Harley into the back seat. The dog grumbled but hopped into the back.

Ella took time to greet Harley before settling into her seat. Ryder shut the door and went around to get into the driver's seat.

"So how was work?" he asked.

"We were unusually busy this morning. Three separate homeschool groups came in for research materials, and Mrs. Hollister returned her romance novels and pretended she doesn't read them for the spicy scenes." She laughed. "But when I tried to steer her toward sweeter stories, she scolded me, saying she might be eighty but she wasn't ready to be put out to pasture yet."

Ryder chuckled. "I think she taught both my parents when they were in elementary school."

"What about you? How are things at the Stargazer?"

"Cold. Demanding. Beautiful." He paused, considering what to say, but for some reason he wanted to be completely honest with her about ranching life. In the past, he'd always considered the ranch separate from his dating life. But Ella McIntyre was different. As he was finding out. "Found a heifer we'd been missing this morning in the east ravine."

"That doesn't sound like a happy reunion."

"It wasn't," he said simply.

"I'm sorry, Ryder." Ella's voice softened, and she reached over to touch his arm briefly.

He briefly glanced at her before turning his attention back to his driving. "It's a fact of life. Especially on a ranch. On a brighter note, I've convinced Dad and the others to let me convert two hundred acres to organic this spring. The premium on grass-fed, organic beef makes the certification process worth it."

"That sounds like a big undertaking."

"It is," he agreed. "But the ranch needs to evolve if it's going to survive. My great-grandfather wouldn't recognize half of what we do now, but the core is the same—good land management, healthy animals, sustainable practices."

"Listen to you, sounding like a businessman instead of a cowboy."

He could feel the warmth of her smile on him and was glad he'd confided in her. "Can't I be both?"

"I suppose you can." She paused. "It's impressive. What you've done with the Stargazer. Your dad must be so proud."

"I haven't done it alone. It's a family business. We're in it together."

"I know, and I'm jealous," she said in a wistful tone.

"Jealous?" His foot eased off the gas pedal and he took his eyes off the highway to glance at her. "Why?"

"Your family supports what you're doing, the choices you've made."

"Yours hasn't?" He found that hard to believe. She was so dedicated and was doing a lot for Tenacity and its citizens.

"They were disappointed that I didn't want to leave Tenacity and use my degree somewhere more 'prestigious,'" she said, putting air quotes around the last word.

"Ah, yes, prestigious." Janelle had used words like that. He reached over and briefly touched her thigh. "I think what you're doing can be life-changing for the people of Tenacity, and if that's not prestigious, I don't know what is."

"Thank you. Not everyone understands why I do this—why I stay in a town that can barely afford to keep the library operating."

"That's where you're most needed," Ryder said and meant it.

In the beginning, he had questioned her dedication to staying in Tenacity, but now he could only regret those doubts. Almost as much as he regretted not kissing her last night.

Hoping to lighten the mood, he told her about some ideas he had for the carnival, featuring games like a black cat ring toss and a plastic pool with lucky and unlucky rubber ducks. Kids could fish for prizes.

Soon they were throwing ideas back and forth, with Ella taking notes and laughing at his some of his outlandish suggestions.

He loved the sound of that laugh and wouldn't mind hearing it for the rest of his life.

*Whoa, cowboy, don't you know the eager calf gets tangled in the rope?*

Ryder ordered his mind back onto the carnival plans, hoping that was safer territory. Safer than thinking about missed opportunities to kiss Ella.

Ella tried to concentrate on the carnival plans, but her mind kept going back to the previous conversation. Ryder hadn't denigrated her for staying in Tenacity as her parents had done. She wasn't surprised when he'd asked why she stayed but was definitely surprised he'd applauded her decision.

*Don't let that go to your head,* she cautioned herself, remembering he hadn't kissed her last night. She'd thought for several moments that he was going to, but in the end he hadn't. She was obviously in Ryder's friend zone.

Ryder pulled his truck into the parking lot at the hospital and found a spot. He came around to the passenger side quickly, as if he wanted to help her from the truck, and Ella slowed her progress to let him. She had removed her gloves during the trip and noticed Ryder wasn't wearing his. She readied herself for the small jolt she knew she'd feel if he took her hand.

He assisted her out of the pickup, and she glanced at him to see if he reacted to their skin-on-skin contact. Did a muscle in his cheek tighten as he grasped her hand or was that wishful thinking? Before she could decide, he let go of her to open the rear door to let Harley out of the truck.

"Sit," he said as Harley jumped down.

Ryder reached into the truck and pulled out a red

vest with a giant patch that said Therapy Dog in Training to put on Harley.

Curious, Ella asked if that was necessary.

"I'm not sure, but Renee assures me he met the requirements." He finished securing the vest. "If we were in Tenacity, I wouldn't worry about it, but we're not well-known here."

He pulled out a small shopping bag and handed it to her. "Some more books for the kids."

"That's so sweet of you," she said, and he just grunted and turned toward the edge of the parking lot.

"I'll let Harley relieve himself before we go in," Ryder said and headed toward over to a patch of grass on one side of the hospital parking lot.

"Okay, Harley, you know what to do," Ryder said.

Harley sniffed around and quickly found a satisfactory spot.

"Wow, you have him well trained," Ella said.

"Actually, I had nothing to do with it. Harley was a soldier. He's good at following orders," he said before heading toward the entrance, but not before praising the dog for a job well done.

He glanced at her when he praised the dog and answered her quick grin with one of her own. They hadn't said anything, but she knew what he meant by the grin, and she'd bet he did since he met it with one of his own. She recalled how her parents often communicated without saying a word.

*You're on thin ice with that sort of thinking*, she cautioned herself.

## *Chapter Seven*

The automatic doors of the Bronco Valley Hospital parted with a soft hiss as Ryder stepped through, with Harley padding faithfully between them. The dog's therapy vest was spotless, the bright red fabric a stark contrast against his glossy black and tan coat. Ryder reached down to scratch behind the shepherd's ears, and Harley responded with a contented sigh.

"You've got this, buddy," Ryder reassured as they headed toward the main desk.

"He looks pretty chill. You, on the other hand…"

Ryder's shoulders tensed slightly. "Kids just… They see through you, you know? Can't hide anything from them."

"If it helps," Ella said, her voice softening as she placed a hand lightly on his forearm, "you're already their hero for bringing Harley."

Ryder nodded and headed toward the reception desk. "Let's get this show on the road."

Ryder had surprised Ella with his nervousness. He must care what the kids thought. She liked that. She was definitely seeing more sides to him than the flirting, confident cowboy.

The receptionist, a middle-aged woman with bright purple reading glasses perched on her nose, looked up as they approached. Her face broke into a wide smile. "You must be Mr. Trent with Harley. And Ms. McIntyre, right? The children have been talking about nothing else all morning." She reached into a drawer and pulled out three visitor badges. "Dr. Pearson will be down in just a moment to escort you to the pediatric ward."

As if on cue, the elevator dinged, and a tall, handsome man in blue scrubs and a white coat stepped out accompanied by a woman with similar scrubs and a stethoscope around her neck. They both looked as if they'd just stepped off the soundstage of a daytime soap opera.

Ella couldn't help but notice the spark of interest when the woman doctor saw Ryder. Well, she couldn't blame her. Ryder was one hot cowboy. Would he think a doctor sexier than a plain ole librarian?

The woman stepped forward first. "Ryder Trent? I'm Dr. Pearson and this is Dr. Tremblay. Thank you so much for coming." She extended her hand, which Ryder shook firmly. "And this must be Harley." Dr. Pearson knelt down, allowing Harley to sniff her hand before gently scratching under his chin. "He's gorgeous."

"He knows it, too," Ryder replied, the corner of his mouth quirking up. "This is Ella McIntyre. She's here to help, too."

Dr. Tremblay extended his hand to Ella. "Pleasure to meet you, Ella."

Ella shook his hand, noticing he had the whitest teeth

she'd ever seen. Yup, definitely worthy of being on television.

"Ella has Harley in a reading program back in Tenacity," Ryder offered with a quick look at Dr. Tremblay.

Dr. Pearson straightened and shook Ella's hand, too. "The dog reads?"

Ryder laughed. "The kids read to him. Ella arranged it all so kids who need some extra help can feel comfortable practicing their reading."

The doctor nodded. "I think I've heard about something like that. I'm so glad you're here today. The kids could really use some joy right now. If you'll follow me, I'll take you up to the ward."

"Pleasure to meet you, Ella," Dr. Tremblay said and touched Dr. Pearson's arm. "Talk to you later."

As they headed toward the elevator, Ella had a feeling Harley wasn't the only one bringing joy to the hospital. She'd noticed several nurses straining to get a better look at the tall, sexy cowboy walking through their halls.

Maybe they want to get a better look at Harley.

*Yeah, right*, she thought and grinned to herself.

As they entered the elevator, Ryder found himself aware of Ella beside him. When the elevator jolted slightly, she instinctively steadied herself against his arm, and he had to fight the urge to place his hand over hers.

"We have eight children in the pediatric ward currently," Dr. Pearson explained as the elevator ascended. "Ages range from four to thirteen. Some are recovering from surgeries, others are here for treatment of chronic conditions. We've set up a small recreation area where you can interact with them all at once, if that works for you."

"That's fine," Ryder said. He rubbed a hand down his pant leg. He wanted this to go well. He wanted Ella to see he was more than just a serial dater. He refused to examine the importance. For now.

The elevator doors slid open to reveal a brightly painted hallway adorned with colorful murals of mountains, forests and wildlife—a stark contrast to the sterile white walls of the lower floors. Harley's ears perked up at the sound of children's voices drifting from down the hall.

Ella glanced at him as they followed Dr. Pearson.

"I'm sure it will be great," she whispered as if she could sense his nervousness.

"I hope so," he admitted quietly. Then, after a pause: "I'm glad you're here."

The simple confession hung in the air between them, heavier than he'd intended. What got into him when he was with Ella? Her blue eyes met his, and for a moment, he was certain she could see straight through to everything he'd been trying so hard to conceal.

"I wouldn't miss it," she finally replied, her voice just as soft.

The recreation room was awash with natural light from large windows that overlooked the Montana mountains in the distance. Eight children of various ages were seated in a loose semicircle of chairs, some attached to IV poles, others in wheelchairs. Their excited chatter died down as Dr. Pearson entered, followed by Ryder, Ella and Harley.

"Everyone," Dr. Pearson announced, "this is Mr. Trent and Ms. McIntyre and their very special friend, Harley."

A chorus of gasps and exclamations filled the room as the children caught sight of Harley.

"Is he a police dog?" asked a boy of about ten, his head wrapped in bandages.

"No, but he used to be in the army. Now, he's practicing to be a therapy dog," Ryder explained.

"Why does he have to practice?" another boy asked.

Ryder looked to Ella, who smiled and said, "He's just like you. You have to practice baseball or ice skating or maybe the piano to get better at it, don't you?"

All the children nodded and seemed to look at the dog with new respect.

Kneeling down to Harley's level, Ryder said, "He's here to meet all of you. Would you all like a chance to pet him?"

Enthusiastic nods and yeses answered him.

"Before we start," Ella added, stepping forward, "does anyone have questions about Harley or concerns about dogs? It's okay if you do."

Ella glanced at him, and Ryder nodded and smiled, glad she had thought to ask. Renee had said the children were screened before their visit, but sometimes seeing Harley in person might prompt a different response.

A small girl with a nasal cannula raised her hand timidly. "Will he jump on us? My grandma's dog does and it scares me." The girl glanced at the other kids and added, "Only sometimes."

Ella exchanged a glance with Ryder, motioning for him to take this one.

"That's a great question," Ryder said, his voice gentle. "Harley is specially trained not to jump on people, especially kids. He knows he's working right now." He reached for the plastic bag he'd given Ella earlier. She handed it over, and he pulled out a handful of small laminated cards. "These have some rules for meeting Harley. Ms. McIntyre will pass them out, and we can go through them together."

As Ella distributed the cards, her fingers brushed against Ryder's, sending that now-familiar jolt of electricity through him. Their eyes met briefly, and he could have sworn he saw a flush rise to her cheeks before she quickly turned away to hand a card to the nearest child.

For the next hour, Ryder and Ella took turns demonstrating Harley's training. The shepherd sat patiently as each child approached to pet him, his tail thumping steadily against the floor. He performed a series of tricks that elicited squeals of delight: rolling over, playing dead and even gently retrieving a soft toy for a girl in a wheelchair who couldn't reach the floor.

Ryder found himself repeatedly glancing at Ella, captivated by the way she interacted with the children—her genuine laugh, the soft touch of her hand on a shoulder, the attentive way she listened to their stories. Twice their eyes met across the circle, and twice he felt that peculiar tightness in his chest that seemed to appear only in her presence.

"Okay, who wants to see Harley's best trick?" Ryder asked, pulling a treat from his pocket.

"Me!" chorused the children.

"For this one, I need a volunteer." A forest of hands shot up. "How about…you?" He pointed to a solemn-faced boy of about six who hadn't said much during the visit.

The boy's eyes widened in surprise, and he looked uncertainly at the nurse standing beside him.

"It's okay, Ethan," the nurse encouraged. "Mr. Trent and Harley won't hurt you."

Ethan slid cautiously off his chair and approached.

"Harley is going to deliver a special message to you," Ryder explained, taking a small scroll tied with a ribbon from the bag. He attached it to Harley's collar and gave a hand signal. "Deliver, Harley."

The shepherd trotted obediently to Ethan and sat, tilting his head expectantly.

"You can take the scroll," Ella prompted gently when Ethan hesitated.

With trembling fingers, the boy untied the ribbon and unrolled the paper. "It says, 'You are brave,'" he read slowly.

"That's right," Ryder confirmed, moving closer and kneeling beside the boy. "Harley can tell you're very brave. Just like he was when he was in the army."

Ethan's face broke into a tentative smile as he reached out to pet Harley's head. "I am brave," he whispered, more to himself than anyone else.

Ryder felt Ella's presence before he saw her, the

faint scent of vanilla cake preceding her as she knelt on Ethan's other side.

"You know what?" she said to the boy. "Mr. Trent is brave, too. He was nervous about coming to meet all of you today."

"You were?" Ethan asked, looking at Ryder with surprise.

Ryder shot Ella a look of mock betrayal, but nodded. "Absolutely. Being brave doesn't mean you're not scared. It means you do something even when it scares you."

Ethan seemed to consider this deeply, then nodded with newfound wisdom. "Like getting poked with a needle."

"Exactly like that," Ryder agreed and glanced at the dog and back to the boy. "Harley doesn't like going to the doctor, either."

Harley whined and lifted a paw over his face and the children roared with laughter.

"But Dr. Pearson's nice," ventured a young girl, and everyone nodded their heads vigorously.

Ella held the plastic bag up, reminding Ryder they still needed to pass out the presents. Ella broke into a smile when she pulled out the various books. The stories all featured a German shepherd.

"Good one," she whispered to him.

As the visit began to wind down, Dr. Pearson suggested a group photo with Harley. The children gathered around the German shepherd, who sat regally in the center, seemingly aware of his important role. Ryder stood behind them, while Ella positioned herself before the group, ready to take the picture with her phone.

"You should be in it, too," Ryder said, gesturing for her to join them.

"Someone needs to take the photo," she protested.

"I can do that," Dr. Pearson offered, taking the phone from Ella's hand. "Go on, this was your project, too."

Ella hesitantly moved to stand beside Ryder, who instinctively placed his arm around her shoulders to make room in the crowded photo. The casual touch sent warmth spreading through his entire body, and he found himself wishing the moment wouldn't end.

"Everyone say 'Harley'!" Dr. Pearson called.

"Harley!" the children shouted, while the adults smiled and the dog's ears perked up at the sound of his name.

As they said their goodbyes, Ethan approached Ryder one last time and tugged on his sleeve.

"Will you and Ms. McIntyre and Harley come back?" he asked hopefully.

Ryder glanced at Ella, who was busy helping the nurses pass out books appropriate for the age of the patient.

"I'd like that," he said. "If Ms. McIntyre agrees."

"To what?" Ella asked, looking up.

"To another visit," Ryder clarified, suddenly feeling uncharacteristically nervous. "Ethan was asking if we'd visit again."

Something flickered in Ella's expression—surprise, perhaps, or maybe something deeper. "I'd like that, too," she said softly.

As they walked back to the parking lot, Harley trotting between them, a comfortable silence settled around them. The morning sun had given way to afternoon clouds, and a breeze blew through the bare aspens lining the hospital drive.

"Thank you," Ryder said finally. "For coming with me today. It wouldn't have been as much fun without you."

Ella smiled, her eyes lighting up and making his heart skip. "That's what friends are for, right?"

"Right," he agreed, ignoring the pang in his chest at the word *friends*. "Still, you were amazing with those kids. Especially Ethan."

"So were you," she countered. "You have a gift, Ryder Trent. Even if you don't see it yourself."

"What do you mean?"

"You and Harley. I know how busy the ranch keeps you, but you could think about doing things like this on a regular basis or during slow times."

"Not sure there is such a thing as a slow time on a ranch."

"Oh, well, it was just a thought."

"Hey." He reached out and touched her arm. "It's a good thought, but Harley still belongs to Liam Martin, and I know once he gets back to Tenacity, he'll want him back. That was the agreement when I said I'd take care of him."

"That's right. You're such a natural with him, I keep forgetting he's only temporary in your life."

Something about the way she said the word *temporary* stuck in his craw. It was true, but it still bothered him. Maybe because that's how he'd been treating the women in his life ever since Janelle.

"Do you need to get back to Tenacity by a certain time?" Ryder asked after they'd left the hospital parking lot. He didn't want their day together to end yet.

"No. I'm free the rest of the day."

"Want to grab something to eat before we head back? There's a bigger selection of places to choose from than in Tenacity."

"Sounds good. You don't have to get back, do you? I don't want to keep you."

*Keep me, please.* "I know this will sound like I was making excuses before when I said there's no real slow time on the ranch. But there really are slower times and I'm not the only one working it. So it's good."

"I'm glad because I'm getting hungry."

"Food it is. How about Lulu's? In addition to great burgers, they make outstanding milk shakes."

"Ooh, yum."

"I've been thinking about Reading Tails and I will try to keep bringing Harley. At least until Liam gets back."

"Thanks. You know, you could always get your own dog. You seem to enjoy Harley's company."

"I'd have to do a heck of a lot of thinkin' on it before committing to that."

"Of course," she said. "You aren't the commitment type."

He gave her a sharp look. That was true, and he

didn't like hearing that coming from Ella, but he chose to let it drop.

Once they were seated and had ordered, Ella smiled at him from across the table. "Did your parents discourage you from going to college? Is that why you didn't go?"

Ryder stiffened, his heart starting to pound. Why had he thought Ella McIntyre was different? "Why would you ask that?"

She shrugged. "Before I left today my mother called. I guess our conversation is still on my mind."

"Why?" He hated the suspicion in his tone, but he'd been unable to keep it out. At least this time he hadn't been so rash as to declare any deep feelings. At least he could get out of this with his pride intact. As for his heart—

"As usual, she was once again harping on how, with my degree, I should get a better job somewhere else," she said.

He recalled Ella bringing that up earlier today. When would she decide they were right? When would she decide she needed to get out of Nowhere, Montana? Just like Janelle. He cleared his throat. "In their defense, Tenacity isn't exactly a boomtown."

"Not yet. But once the Dinosaur Center opens, things will pick up."

"Do you really think so?" Okay, maybe he'd misread her. He certainly hoped so.

"I know so."

"Let's hope you're right. I know the new mayor seems to think so, and I believe she has Tenacity's best interests at heart." And he wanted Ella to stay. Would that make a difference to her future plans?

The waitress came, and they ordered burgers and fries with milkshakes.

While they waited for their food, Ella asked him questions about the ranch and ranching life.

"You could come and I could put you to work," he teased, but deep down he wondered if she'd like ranch life. Would she fit in at the Stargazer? Janelle would have scoffed at the very idea.

Ella grinned at him and took a sip. "I might just take you up on that, cowboy."

"Any time, librarian. Any time," he said, returning her smile.

The waitress brought juicy burgers piled high with lettuce, tomato slices and onions.

"So, did your parents want you to stay to work the ranch?" Ella asked after several bites of her burger. "Is that why you didn't go to college?"

He might as well tell her the truth. The whole truth. "I chose not to go."

"Why?"

He looked straight at her. If he was going to do this, he was going to do it right. "I barely graduated high school."

She drew her head back. "Really? I find that hard to believe."

"Believe it."

"Care to explain?"

Not really, but he'd made up his mind to be truthful. He wanted to know if this was going to make a difference. So he'd treat it like a Band-Aid and just rip it off. "I have a learning disability that made school a nightmare."

"Dyslexia?"

"No. That might have been easier for everyone to understand. It took a while, but I was finally diagnosed with dysgraphia." If not for the persistence of his parents he might have gone undiagnosed and continued to be labeled as lazy and uncaring. "It's not as well-known but it—"

"I'm familiar with it."

"You are?"

"I researched it when one of the boys in Story Time was having problems. Luckily, it was recognized early and he's receiving coping strategies."

"That's good. I wasn't quite that fortunate. By the time I got help, I was pretty much done with school. High school was a nightmare academically."

"I can imagine. I admire you for getting that far without coping strategies. And you've created a successful career. You should be very proud of all that you've accomplished."

"Career?" he questioned before he could think better of it. Was he opening a can of worms by revealing too much? Janelle certainly hadn't considered ranching a career. At least not one worthy of her.

"I'm not so sure about that..." he began, thinking of the things Janelle had said and thought about him. She hadn't seemed to think he was much of a success. He shook his head. Why had he let her get into his head and mess with it like that?

"I am."

Ella's statement broke into his thoughts and, for a moment, Ryder was lost. He tried to gather the threads of their conversation. "You are?"

"I am." She reached across the table and placed her hand on his. "You've kept the Stargazer Ranch going despite all the downturns in the economy. That's something to be proud of."

Her simple touch warmed his blood as her words touched his heart. "It's my family's legacy. I wasn't going to be the one to let it fail."

"And you've succeeded. Look at how many family-run farms and ranches have gone under. And having a successful ranch here helps the community. Tenacity may be a dot on the map, but to the people who live here, it's pretty important."

"You sound like you really like it here." Looking back, he realized Janelle had always had one foot out the door. Maybe what happened was just as much about her as him. He'd never thought of it like that. Had he really been placing the blame on himself for not being what *she* wanted?

"Why would you be surprised that I like it here?"

"With your degree and all, I guess I thought you'd *want* to go elsewhere."

"Even when I was away at university, I always planned on coming back here if at all possible. I had to leave to get my degree, but that didn't mean I wanted to leave permanently. As soon as the Tenacity library had an opening, I jumped at it. Everything fell into place, like it was meant to be. My parents were leaving, so I moved into the house where I grew up."

"Well, I'm glad you moved back."

"And I'm glad you're still here. What made you think staying here and running the family ranch wasn't a valid career option?"

His first impulse was to change the subject, but he wanted to be honest with Ella. She deserved that much from him. "Something somebody said."

"They were wrong. Got that, cowboy?"

"Got it," he said and tried to mean it.

## *Chapter Eight*

The snowshoes Ella had been so excited about now looked more like medieval torture devices. She'd tried walking in them back at the ranch house—without much success—so Ryder had suggested they drive to the spot he'd said would be a good place to try and see the northern lights.

Now, Ryder knelt before her, helping to secure the complicated straps around her winter boots. While the image of Ryder kneeling before her conjured up all sorts of imaginative scenarios, Ella kept telling herself to concentrate on the task at hand.

"Trust me," he said, looking up with that crooked smile that never failed to make her stomach flip. "You'll get the hang of it in no time."

The February air bit at her cheeks, but she barely noticed the cold with Ryder's body so close to hers. His touch was gentle yet confident, like everything else about him. The man was utterly in his element out here in the Montana wilderness, while she suddenly felt like an awkward intruder in the pristine landscape.

"There," he said, giving the final strap a practiced

tug. “Try standing up. Keep your feet shoulder-width apart.”

She gripped his offered forearms, grabbing onto solid muscle beneath his shearling jacket, and wobbled to her feet. The snowshoes felt impossibly huge and unwieldy, like she’d strapped tennis rackets to her boots.

“I feel ridiculous,” she admitted, still clutching his arms.

“You look adorable.” His voice was a deep baritone that sent a shiver down her spine—one that had nothing to do with the temperature. “Ready to try walking?”

“Do I have a choice?”

“Well, you’re the one who said you wanted to see the northern lights.” His eyes crinkled at the corners. “And the forecast tonight is perfect for it. Clear skies, strong solar activity… We just need to get to my favorite viewpoint up on the ridge.”

The moon painted the snow-covered landscape in ethereal silver, making the wilderness look like something out of a fairy tale. Pine trees cast long shadows across the untouched powder, their branches heavy with snow. In the distance, the jagged peaks of the rugged Montana mountains pierced the star-studded sky.

“Okay, walking in snowshoes is just like regular walking, but with a wider stance,” Ryder explained. “Lift your foot, move it forward and plant it down. The snowshoe will keep you on top of the snow instead of sinking in.”

He demonstrated, making it look effortless as he took a few steps away. She tried to mimic his movement, but her first step resulted in the front of the snowshoe catching in the snow, nearly sending her face-first into a drift.

Ryder's strong hands caught her before she could fall. "I've got you," he murmured, his breath warm against her ear. "Try again. I won't let you fall."

Something in his tone made her wonder if he was still just talking about snowshoeing.

With his steady presence beside her, she slowly found her rhythm. Step, lift, plant. Step, lift, plant. The squeak of compressed snow beneath the aluminum frames became almost meditative. Soon they were making their way along the moonlit trail that wound through the towering pines, their breath forming silver clouds in the crisp air.

"You're a natural," Ryder said, his voice warm with approval.

She snorted. "You're a liar, but a sweet one."

"I mean it. You should have seen me the first time I tried this. Spent more time eating snow than walking on it."

"You?" She shot him a skeptical look.

"Everyone's a beginner sometime." He shrugged, then added more quietly, "At everything."

Ella sensed they'd been dancing around something since Ryder had walked into the library with his sister. Her heart raced every time he looked at her with those intense blue eyes.

The trail began to climb, and she had to focus on breathing as she ascended. Except for her college years, Ella had lived in Montana all her life and had dressed appropriately in layers. Ryder had supplied her with a headlamp. "Not all night creatures are as wonderful as your friend Awesome," he'd explained.

"Almost there," Ryder said after about forty minutes of hiking. "Just around this bend."

They emerged from the trees into a small clearing at the top of the ridge, and Ella gasped. The valley spread out below her like a silver-dusted painting, the moonlight catching every crystal of snow. The surrounding peaks seemed close enough to touch, their rugged faces etched in stark relief against the star-strewn sky. How had she missed this despite living in Montana all her life?

"Ryder, this is…" Words failed her.

"Worth the climb?" He moved so he was standing beside her, his shoulder brushing hers.

"Absolutely." She turned to thank him and found him already looking at her, his expression soft in the moonlight. Her breath caught in her throat.

"Look," he whispered, pointing northward.

At first, she saw nothing but stars. Then a faint green ribbon appeared, rippling across the sky like a diaphanous curtain caught in a celestial breeze. As they watched, it grew stronger, dancing and swirling in shades of emerald and mint. Another band joined it, this one with hints of purple at its edges.

"Oh my God," she breathed. "I've never seen anything so beautiful."

"I have."

She turned to find Ryder's gaze fixed on her instead of the sky, intense and unguarded. Her heart thundered against her ribs as he slowly raised one gloved hand to brush a strand of hair from her face.

"Ella," he said, her name barely more than a whisper. "I can't stop thinking about you. And I don't want to."

The aurora painted his face in shifting patterns of green and gold as he cupped her cheek with his hand. She leaned into his touch, no longer feeling the cold at all.

Before she realized what she was doing, she rose up—no small feat in snowshoes—and pressed her lips to his. He made a soft sound of surprise before wrapping his arms around her, pulling her closer. His kiss was like him—gentle but confident, wild but controlled. He tasted of mint and coffee and something essentially Ryder, and she knew with sudden clarity that her life had just irrevocably changed course.

When they finally parted, both slightly breathless, the aurora still danced overhead. But she barely noticed it anymore, too captivated by the way Ryder's eyes shone in the moonlight and the feeling of his strong arms around her.

It was as if she'd been waiting all her life for this moment. For him.

"We should probably head back," he said eventually, though he made no move to release her. "It's getting colder."

She nodded, but neither moved for several long moments. Finally, reluctantly, she pulled away and they began the journey back. The descent was easier than the climb, and she found herself moving with more confidence in the snowshoes.

"You really are a natural," Ryder said, watching her navigate a particularly steep section.

This time, she didn't argue. Because maybe he was right—not just about the snowshoes, but about everything. Could she trust her heart to a playboy cowboy? Did she want to take that chance?

The moon continued its arc across the sky as they made their way down the trail, and she couldn't help but smile. Whatever happened next, Ella knew she would never forget this night—the crunch of snow beneath their feet, the whisper of wind through the pines, the dance of the aurora overhead and the warm pressure of Ryder's hand in hers, guiding her home.

"Damn it all," Ryder muttered, causing Thunder to flick an ear back in curiosity. The horse was used to Ryder's one-sided conversations during their morning rides. This morning was no different. "Can't even go an hour without thinking about her."

And now, since that kiss two nights ago, it was even worse.

If only the carnival had just been another community project—something his sister Cassie had volunteered him for. "You need to use your charm for good, Ryder," she'd teased. "Everyone loves you. Help Ella save the library."

So he had agreed to tag along with Cassie to the library that first day. And yeah, okay, he'd been curious after glimpsing Ella in her red cowgirl boots. Hey, he was a guy, so sue him.

But Cassie had changed her tune in a hurry after

he'd expressed an interest in Ella. What he hadn't told Cassie was how watching Ella's quick mind work—the way her eyes lit up when describing her vision for the carnival, the serious furrow of her brow when checking budget numbers, the unexpected throaty laugh when he cracked a joke—would leave him thinking about her long after they'd said good-night.

Thunder snorted impatiently, pulling Ryder back to the present. He guided the horse toward the cattle, clicking his tongue to start moving the herd.

"I know what you're thinking," he told the horse. "That I'm a damn fool." Thunder tossed his head as if in agreement. "She's way out of my league."

The words from his last conversation with his dad echoed in his head. They'd been mending fences.

"I hear you've been seeing that librarian. I believe her name is Ella," Dad had said as he wound the barbed wire back on itself.

"I've been helping with the fundraiser they're planning," he'd replied, focusing intently on cutting the next length of wire.

"You like her?"

"Everyone likes Ella. She's saving the town's library and helping saving the town itself by working to get the Dinosaur Center opened."

His dad nodded. "Your mom says she's not like the women you usually date."

"Meaning what exactly?" He'd felt a flash of defensiveness.

"Your mom says she's bookish. Maybe a little naive about men."

Ryder knew that his dad was also concerned but using Ryder's mom as an excuse to bring up the topic.

"I'm not sure where you're going with this," Ryder said, trying not to take offense at his dad's concerns.

"We just don't want to see you hurt again," his dad had said and then completely changed the subject.

Ryder winced at the memory as he guided the herd toward the gate. Janelle. Three years had passed since she'd handed back his engagement ring, but the humiliation still burned. Yeah, his dad wasn't so far off the mark with that one.

"I need someone with ambition," she'd said. "Someone who wants more than just this town, this ranch. Someone who challenges me intellectually."

The cattle lowed as they moved through the gate, their breath creating a fog around them. One stubborn heifer tried breaking from the group, and Ryder expertly guided Thunder to head her off.

That was the thing about ranching. It might not require the college degree he'd never earned—not with the dysgraphia that had turned his schoolwork into frustrating jumbles—but it demanded intelligence of a different kind. Problem-solving. Strategy. Reading the land and the weather and the animals. None of which had impressed Janelle.

Did it impress Ella?

The thought ambushed him as he closed the gate behind the last of the cattle. Ella, with her master's degree and her discussions about classic literature he pretended to know more about than he did. Ella, who'd somehow gotten him to volunteer not just his time but his limited skills to build carnival game booths.

"She said she admired me for working the ranch and making it a success," he told Thunder as they headed toward the barn. "She was into that kiss, but that's a long way from being interested in long term."

Was *he* interested in long term?

Thunder's hooves crunched through the snow as they approached the barn. The morning sun now fully illuminated the sprawling property where he'd grown up and the land he loved.

As he dismounted and led Thunder into the warm barn, his phone vibrated in his pocket. Peeling off a glove, he fished it out, his heart giving a ridiculous jump when he saw Ella's name on the screen.

A text message: Morning! Sorry for the early text, but we've got a carnival crisis. The high school band canceled for providing the music. Any chance you know someone musical? Volunteers meeting at 4 today. Hope you can make it.

Ryder leaned against Thunder's stall, reading the message twice. Professional. Friendly. Nothing to suggest she'd woken thinking about him the way he'd spent his morning thinking about her.

"What do you think, boy?" he asked the horse as he began removing the saddle for a rubdown. "Should I tell her about Pete's bluegrass band?"

Thunder snorted, shaking his mane.

"Yeah, you're right. Pete would love the exposure." He typed a quick reply about his friend's band, adding that he'd be at the meeting.

As he finished caring for Thunder and moved on to the morning feeding routine, Ryder found himself wondering what Ella was doing right now. Probably already at the library, arranging books and planning programs that expanded minds. Meanwhile, here he was, shoveling feed and mucking stalls.

"Ryder! There you are." The voice of his brother, Noah, echoed through the barn. "Been looking all over. The feed delivery is here early, and there's a problem with the invoice."

Reality—and responsibility—called. Ryder pocketed his phone and pushed thoughts of Ella aside. He had a ranch to run, cattle to manage and employees who depended on him. No time for daydreaming about a woman who probably saw him as nothing more than a community volunteer with useful carpentry skills.

Ryder approached his older brother and they did the whole man hug thing with Noah giving him a slap on the back.

"How's Lucy and the boys?" Ryder asked. His brother had triplet boys. There was a time when Ryder had thought better him than me but lately…

"Never a dull moment, that's for sure," Noah said. "The boys have been asking when their uncle is coming to see them again."

"Yeah, I've been meaning to bring Harley over," Ryder said. It wasn't as if he had far to go. Noah and Lucy lived on their own spread on the Stargazer Ranch with Noah's three boys.

"That's right. You've been taking care of that dog.

How's it going?" Noah asked as they strode toward the feed truck.

"Great. He loves kids and I bet you boys would love him."

"I'm sure they would but don't give them any ideas, please. You do realize that with triplets we have to get everything times three."

Ryder chuckled but before he could say anything else, Noah asked, "What's this I hear about you and the lady librarian?"

"Just helping out with the fundraising carnival for the library," Ryder said.

"Uh-huh," Noah said with a grin.

Luckily the delivery driver approached with a clipboard before Noah could say anything more.

Ryder was glad to have avoided any conversation about Ella but couldn't help the small smile that crept onto his face at the thought of her. At least he'd see her at four o'clock.

He pulled into the library parking lot fifteen minutes early and grabbed the folder containing the sketches he'd made of the game booths from the passenger seat and headed inside. The blast of warm air as he entered the library was welcome after the cold walk from the parking lot. The familiar scent of books and the faint citrus aroma of cleaning products greeted him, along with the distant sound of Ella's voice from the meeting room at the back.

He followed the sound, pausing in the doorway. Ella stood alone, phone pressed to her ear, gesturing animatedly as she paced. Her wavy hair was pulled up in its usual practical bun, but a few strands had escaped to frame her face. She wore a light blue sweater that complemented her blue eyes, paired with a denim skirt and those red boots, making her look both professional and sexy. At least to him.

"Yes, I understand it's last-minute," she was saying, professional patience evident in her tone. "But we're really in a bind here… That would be wonderful! Thank you so much. I'll email the details right away."

She ended the call with a triumphant "Yes!" and a little fist pump that made Ryder chuckle. The sound alerted her to his presence, and her eyes widened in surprise before a smile spread across her face—a genuine, pleased-to-see-him smile that sent a warmth through his chest that had nothing to do with the library's heating system.

"Ryder. You're early." She tucked her phone into her pocket. "I just solved our music crisis. The elementary school choir director is going to have the kids perform a few songs to open the carnival."

"That's great," he said, stepping into the room and setting his folder on the table. "But I already got my friend Pete and his bluegrass band. He's pretty excited about it. I texted you."

"Oh!" Her face fell slightly. "I didn't see your text. My phone's been going crazy today."

"No problem. We could have both," Ryder suggested quickly, not wanting to see her smile fade. "Kids open the carnival, band plays later?"

The smile returned, brighter this time. "That's perfect. A full day of entertainment." She moved closer, genuine enthusiasm in her eyes. "This carnival is really coming together, isn't it? And a lot of that is thanks to you."

"Me? I'm just building some booths and manning the kissing booth."

She shook her head. "The library wouldn't stand a chance without you."

Something in her earnest expression made Ryder's chest tighten. Did she really see him that way? As someone valuable, someone who contributed something meaningful beyond his reputation as Tenacity's most eligible bachelor?

"It's important to you," he said simply. "So it became important to me."

Their eyes locked, and for a moment, the air between them seemed charged with something unspoken. Ella's cheeks flushed slightly, and Ryder found himself instinctively moving closer.

The library door opened with a distant chime, breaking the spell as voices approached the meeting room.

"Sounds like the others are arriving," Ella said softly, stepping back and tucking a loose strand of hair behind her ear. Was he imagining the slight tremor in her hand?

"Yeah, we should get ready for the meeting," Ryder agreed, knowing Cassie would be among the arrivals. He didn't want to give his sister anything more to bust his butt about.

But as the room filled with people, Ryder couldn't shake the feeling that something had shifted between them since the night they'd kissed. A possibility had opened, as fragile and promising as the first green shoots after a hard winter.

And despite everything—his reputation, his insecurities, his sister's warnings—Ryder found himself hoping it might grow into something more.

Ella mentally kicked herself for not saying anything about that kiss.

And what would she say? *Can we do it again?*

It had been spontaneous. Did he now regret it? Or was she just one of the many women he flirted with and kissed? Did this feel like more because she wanted it to be more? So many questions, but now was not the time nor was this the setting.

"I want to thank you again for the snowshoe lesson and the opportunity to see the aurora," she said before the others arrived.

"And I thank you for inviting me to supper. I had a great time."

"Would you like to come again?" Oh my! Where did *that* come from? "I… I—"

"I'd love to, but how about if I pick you up and we go somewhere? I'd hate for you to have to rush home after this to make supper."

She swallowed hard and decided to take the bull by the horns. "You mean like a date?"

"That's exactly what I mean," he said as others piled into the conference room.

For the rest of the meeting, Ella did her best to keep her mind on the plans for the carnival, but her gaze kept finding its way to Ryder.

This time there was no mistaking what was happening. She and Ryder were dating.

Later that night, Ella glanced at the clock on her kitchen wall for what felt like the hundredth time. Seven forty-five. Ryder was an hour and fifteen minutes late. He'd told her he'd made a reservation in Bronco, but now they wouldn't make it. Had he changed his mind?

"So much for our big date," she muttered to herself, tucking a strand of her hair behind her ear. She'd even worn something sexy from her second drawer. Now she felt silly for having gone to such lengths.

She reached for her phone again, checking for missed calls or texts. Nothing. Even in the short time she'd known him, she'd say this was unlike Ryder.

Just as she was about to call him again, headlights swept across her front window and her heart leaped despite her frustration. She moved to the door, watching through the glass as Ryder's mud-splattered truck pulled into her driveway. The porch light illuminated his tall frame as he hurried toward her door, his gait betraying a slight limp that hadn't been there this afternoon.

When she opened the door, her irritation gave way to concern. Ryder stood on her porch looking nothing like the put-together rancher she'd been expecting. His pants were muddied from the knees down, one leg sporting a long tear. Most alarmingly, there was a scratch across his left cheekbone that had just barely stopped bleeding.

"Ella, I'm so sorry," he said, his deep voice gruff with what sounded like genuine remorse. His blue eyes, usually crinkled at the corners with good humor, were heavy with apology.

She stepped back, allowing him inside. "What happened to you? I've been worried sick. I tried calling and it kept going to voice mail."

Ryder removed his hat, running a hand through his hair, dislodging a small leaf. "I know, I know. My phone's in my truck, dead as a doornail. I would've gone home to clean up first, but then I'd have been even later, and I couldn't bear the thought of standing you up any longer."

The scent of pine and cold February air clung to him as he stepped into her warm entryway.

"You look like you wrestled a bear," she said. She refrained from telling him how she'd started convincing herself that he'd changed his mind and wasn't coming. "Are you hurt?"

Ryder's shoulders slumped as he shook his head. "Not really. Just a few scratches and a bruised ego." He paused, looking uncertain, which was unusual for a man who typically exuded quiet confidence. "I can explain, if you'll let me. But I'll understand if you just want me to leave."

# *Chapter Nine*

Something in his expression—vulnerability mixed with determination—made Ella sigh. She wanted to doctor that cheek, take care of him, whereas about twenty minutes ago she'd been thinking the opposite, but it was obvious something had happened, and her anger and frustration dissolved immediately.

"Why would I want you to leave? Let's get you cleaned up a bit while you tell me what's going on." She gestured toward the kitchen.

"Let me get these boots off. I don't want to track muck across your hardwood."

"I have a first aid kit under the sink in the powder room," she called over her shoulder as she went down the hall. "Sit down in the kitchen and I'll get something to take care of that scratch."

Ryder settled into one of Ella's kitchen chairs with a slight wince, more from what was coming than from any physical injury. He was going to have to tell her what had happened. Even if it made him look like a damn fool.

She came into the kitchen carrying a red plastic box

with a white cross on it. Setting it on the table next to Ryder, she opened it and took out several items.

"Is this really necessary?" he asked.

"Yes," she said with a narrow-eyed look.

He grinned. She hadn't quite pulled off the look. "Then have at it, Nurse Ella."

He winced as she dabbed the antiseptic onto his cheek. Her touch was gentle, but the sting made his eyes water all the same. *Toughen up*, he ordered himself.

"Hold still," she murmured, her face so close to his that he could count each freckle scattered across her nose and cheeks. "This cut isn't too deep, but it's right along your cheekbone."

"It's nothing," he said, trying not to focus on how her lips pursed in concentration. "You should see the other guy."

"Ryder Trent, you're not going to tell me you were in a fight with someone." She pulled back abruptly and glared at him. "Is that what you're telling me?"

He sighed, knowing he needed to come clean. Anyway, the story had a happy ending for the other guy. Glancing at Ella, and despite the current glare, he decided he was getting a happy ending, too.

"No. No fight. It was all my own doing," he admitted.

She frowned. "So tell me what happened."

"I was on my way here when I spotted something on the side of the road."

"Something?" She swallowed, the hand that had been tending to his injuries suspended in midair.

He reached out and wrapped his hand around her

wrist. “It was a possum, but it wasn’t Awesome. It didn’t have that dark patch on its back.”

She heaved a sigh of relief, but her face still reflected sadness. “Was it…?”

“At first I thought it was.” He entwined his fingers with hers. “I decided I couldn’t just leave it. So I stopped, thinking the least I could do was bury it.”

“It’s February. In Montana. The ground is frozen,” she pointed out.

He chuckled, shaking his head. “I didn’t say I’d thought it through.”

“You said at first you thought it was dead. What happened?”

“Turns out it wasn’t dead. Just playing possum.”

She shook her head. “They don’t play. It they get scared, they shut down or faint.”

“Like those fainting goats?” he asked, and she nodded, so he continued, “Anyway, I put my gloves on and picked it up.”

“Do you think he was okay?” she asked, her tone showing her concern.

“It appeared to be. I don’t know what caused it to faint or whatever the heck it was doing.” He tried to shrug but froze when her fingers pressed firmly against his jaw, holding him steady.

“Don’t move,” she warned, carefully placing a butterfly bandage across his cut. “Please continue with your story.”

He swallowed hard. Her scent—that vanilla birthday cake stuff she used—made it difficult to concentrate.

“Next thing I knew I had a wriggling, hissing creature in my hands." He shook his head at the memory. "I didn't want to just drop it and risk hurting it, so I started into the woods, but I ended up slipping and falling on my butt. I lost my grip on him and he took off into the woods."

She pursed her lips as if suppressing laughter.

"Go ahead and laugh. I wasn't sure who was more startled when I picked him up, me or him."

"Startled or not, I'm sure he was grateful for your assistance." Ella's laugh was soft and musical and the affection in her teasing tone made his chest tighten.

"Yeah, right."

"So when you said 'you should see the other guy' you meant a terrified opossum?"

"Hey now, he may have been terrified, but that little fella had a lot of fight in him." Ryder attempted to maintain his dignity, which was challenging sitting on a kitchen chair while Ella tended to his wound. He was never going to live this down.

"This is all your fault. I pulled over because I know how much you like those little critters," he grumbled but ruined the effect with a grin.

"My hero," she said with a sigh that did funny things to his insides.

"Some hero. The little monster let me pick it up before it hissed at me and took off into the woods when I fell." Ryder closed his eyes briefly, remembering the ridiculousness of what followed. "It was dark, and I was still worried it might be hurt, so I followed it."

"Into the woods. In February. In Montana." Ella's

eyebrows rose as she reached for a second butterfly bandage.

"It sounds worse when you say it like that," he admitted.

"Please continue." Her eyes sparkled with amusement. "I'm dying to know how this ends with you bleeding."

Ryder rubbed the back of his neck. "Well, there I was, traipsing through two feet of snow, following possum tracks in the twilight like some deranged wilderness guide—"

"As one does."

"—and I lost sight of him in this thicket. I pushed through some branches, and that's when I heard it." He paused for dramatic effect.

Ella leaned closer, her breath warm against his face. "Heard what?"

"The most ungodly, demonic hissing sound you've ever heard. And then something flew at my face."

Her eyes widened. "I don't believe it. The opossum attacked you?"

"No. Worse. I'd disturbed a grouse that was sheltering in the thicket. Damn thing exploded out right at me, and I stumbled backward, tripped over a log hidden under the snow and..." He gestured to his face. "Caught my cheek on a branch on the way down."

Ella pressed her lips together, clearly fighting laughter.

"Go ahead," he said dryly. "Laugh it up."

She lost the battle, giggles bubbling out of her as she

pressed the second bandage in place. "I'm sorry. Did you ever find the possum again?"

"Oh yeah," Ryder said, lips twitching despite himself. "After I picked myself up and stopped the bleeding with my bandanna, I spotted it watching me from up in a tree. I swear it was smirking."

"They're intelligent creatures," Ella said.

"Ha-ha."

She was still standing between his legs as he sat on the chair, her hands resting lightly on his shoulders. The humor in her eyes softened to something else, something that made his mouth go dry.

"I named him," Ryder confessed, his voice rougher than he intended. Why in the world had he confessed that?

"You named the possum?" Her fingers tightened slightly on his shoulders.

"Oscar. Oscar O. Possum." He felt ridiculous saying it, but the smile that bloomed across her face was worth it.

"That's actually adorable," she said, then bit her lip. The gesture drew his gaze, and the atmosphere in the kitchen shifted, the air suddenly thicker.

Ryder cleared his throat. "So, uh, about that dinner reservation…"

"I think you've had enough adventure for one night," Ella said, but she didn't step back. If anything, she moved closer, the fabric of her sweater brushing against his chest. "Besides, you're still bleeding a little."

"Am I?" His voice was barely above a whisper.

She nodded, reaching up to touch the corner of the

bandage. "I could cook something here instead. I froze some chili last time I made it. I can thaw it in the microwave, and I can make some biscuits and salad if that's okay with you."

He should probably insist on taking her out as planned. But the thought of staying here, in the warm cocoon of her kitchen while the snow fell outside, was too tempting to resist.

"That sounds perfect," he said, reaching up to capture her hand where it hovered near his cheek. "But only if you let me help."

"Deal." Her smile was soft, her eyes meeting his with an intensity that made his heart hammer against his ribs. "Though I'm not sure I should trust you in the kitchen given your track record today."

"Very funny." Impulsively, he tugged gently on her hand, pulling her even closer. Her expression grew serious, the teasing light in her eyes transforming into something deeper as she allowed herself to be drawn in.

"Your poor face," she murmured, her free hand coming up to trace the uninjured side of his cheek. "Does it hurt much?"

"Not anymore," he said honestly. How could anything hurt when she was looking at him like that?

For a moment, they stayed frozen in that position—Ryder seated on the chair, Ella standing between his legs, their faces inches apart. He could feel the rapid beat of her pulse under his fingers where they circled her wrist. The only sounds were the soft hiss of the radiator and the distant ticking of a clock.

“I should…” she began, then swallowed. “I should get the chili out of the freezer.”

“Right,” he agreed, but neither of them moved.

“Ryder,” she said softly, his name a question and an answer all at once.

“Yeah?” His other hand came up to rest lightly on her hip, giving her plenty of opportunity to step away if she wanted to.

She didn’t. Instead, she leaned in slightly, her gaze dropping to his mouth. “I’m really glad Oscar is okay.”

A laugh rumbled up from his chest. “Me, too.”

And then she was smiling against his lips as she closed the final distance between them, and Ryder decided that maybe, just maybe, his wildlife rescue mission hadn’t been such a disaster after all.

As with their first kiss, Ella was swept up in a maelstrom of emotions. She might not have a lot of experience with the opposite sex, but she knew what she liked. And she liked having Ryder’s lips on hers.

She may have initiated the kiss by putting her lips against his, but he soon took charge. His lips were firm and gentle, coaxing a response from her, and she parted her lips, letting his tongue slide against hers. She couldn’t control the small sigh that escaped at the intimate contact.

Despite how wonderful the kiss felt, their positions made it awkward, and as she tried to move closer, her elbow caught the bottle of antiseptic and knocked it over. Ryder managed to grab the bottle before all its contents spilled out, but in doing so he had to break contact.

"Thanks," she said in a breathless tone.

"For saving the bottle or for the kiss?"

"Both," she said with a grin.

A slow smile spread across Ryder's face. "So you're not mad about missing supper in Bronco?"

Ella shook her head, feeling something inside her blossom. "How could I be mad when you've just shown me exactly who you are? A man who would go to ridiculous lengths to honor something important to me, even when no one was watching."

He could have driven past the animal and not even told her what he'd seen. She would have been none the wiser.

The air between them seemed to thicken, charged with something deeper than the casual affection they'd been flirting with. Ryder turned his hand beneath hers, lacing their fingers together.

"I don't mind chasing wild possums for you, Ella McIntyre," he said, his voice low and serious.

She believed him. Moreover, she suddenly knew with startling clarity that she would do the same for him. That somewhere between the day Cassie dragged him into the library and this evening, she'd begun falling for Ryder Trent. She didn't want to give it a name yet because it was still too new.

To help distract her from those thoughts and to prevent her from blurting out something she might regret, she pulled away and straightened up. She didn't want ill-timed words to come between them. Once feelings were revealed, it would be difficult to take those words back and keep her pride intact.

"Most people would think it's strange, me getting attached to a wild possum," she said as she began putting items back into the first aid kit.

Ryder stood and collected the used gauze pads to throw in the trash. "I don't think it's strange."

"You don't?"

"No." He reached out, tucking a strand of hair behind her ear. "I think it's kind. Compassionate."

A small smile tugged at her lips. "We're not going there again, are we?"

"I think that kiss proves I feel more than just admiration for you. But I'm not going to apologize for admiring the way you care about things. People. Even possums."

She laughed softly, mainly to disguise the hint of vulnerability she was feeling. Yeah, good call not blurting out feelings. "None of your other girlfriends named possums, I'm guessing."

"No," he admitted. "They didn't."

"I'm not sure that's a compliment."

"The women I've dated before are all nice enough. They enjoyed a good time, but none of them would have noticed a possum in their yard, let alone cared enough to feed it. None of them would have told me about it if they had."

"Do you prefer it that way?"

Ryder took a deep breath. "I thought I did, but…"

Not wanting him to see the hurt she wasn't sure she could hide, she started to turn away but he caught her arm.

Turning her back to face him, he said, "That was

then. This is now. I enjoy the conversations we have. I enjoy spending time with you. I couldn't imagine teaching any of the other women how to snowshoe. I can't imagine any of them wanting to learn. Promise not to change, Ella."

"I promise."

"But there is one thing," he said. "I don't know about you, but I'm starving. Wrangling possums takes a lot of energy."

"Oh, that's right. I promised you some supper. Let me pull the chili out of the freezer."

"And that reminds me, I do have something for you in the truck. Let me go get it."

"I'll start supper while you do that."

"I'll help as soon as I get back in."

Ryder slipped his feet into his boots but didn't bother with his jacket as he went back to his truck. He needed some time to cool off. Tonight's bitter cold might help clear his mind. He'd been close to saying things to Ella that he might regret. She wasn't like Janelle, he knew that now, but he still didn't want to say things that couldn't be unsaid. Things that might hang in the air between them. That wasn't to say things weren't heading that way.

He grabbed the gift bag off the seat and went back to the porch, where he stomped snow and mud off his boots. These used to be his good boots, but he wasn't so sure after tonight. Leaving his footwear by the door, he strode in his socked feet to Ella's kitchen. He stopped for a moment in the doorway and watched her humming as she worked.

She turned and gave him a big smile. Oh man, he'd chase a thousand possums into the woods for that smile.

Ella had put the container of frozen chili in the microwave to defrost and turned on the oven to cook some canned biscuits. Not exactly a fancy supper, but she was glad she had something substantial to offer him.

"I thought you might like this," he said as he stepped into the kitchen with a brightly colored gift bag.

"Thank you," she said and reached for the bag. Her fingers brushed his as she took it, sending a current of warmth up her arm.

He shrugged. "It's no big deal. I saw it and thought of you. I'm hoping you're like most folks in Tenacity and still have a DVD player since our high-speed internet isn't always high speed."

She nodded and pulled out the two DVDs and gasped with genuine delight. "Oh my goodness. Where did you get these?"

"I happened to come across them. Thought you might like them."

She shook her head. The DVDs were both PBS documentaries about animals in the wild, both including segments featuring opossums. "You did not just happen across these, Ryder Trent. They're not something you pull off the shelf at the local department store, even if you go all the way to Bozeman. You had to track these down."

"Okay. You caught me. I did some research and

found them on eBay." A bit of color rose on his cheeks. "Although after tonight's adventure, I'm not so sure I made a good choice."

She hugged the packages to her chest and leaned over and gave him a quick kiss. It wasn't a passionate kiss—she'd meant it as a thank-you—but it did have a lot of passionate feelings behind it.

"Okay, I take that back. Everything about tonight has been worth it," he said. Clearing his throat, he continued, "I hope you don't mind me staying and watching them with you."

"Of course. After the service you performed, it's a must."

He chuckled. "I think Oscar would have been fine without my intervention."

She shook her head. "You don't know that. He might have been a sitting duck if a predator like a coyote came along."

"Then I was glad to be of service."

"And I would love to watch them with you." The prospect of sitting beside Ryder on a couch, sharing laughter in the firelight, sent a thrill through her. "Would you mind getting a fire going in the fireplace?"

"Sounds like a plan," he said and disappeared back into the living room.

She heaved a deep sigh. Sure, she'd been looking forward to going to a restaurant in Bronco with him tonight, but this might be even better.

And she told him so as they sat side by side on her couch after supper watching nature documentaries.

"Not what I had planned," he said.

"But wonderful nonetheless, unless my chili wa—"

He silenced her with a finger across her lips. "It was delicious. All of it. Even this."

"Even this?"

"Especially this," he said and entwined his fingers with hers as they sat back on the couch. "And to think I used to think I was better with verbal communication."

She gave him a quizzical look and he continued, "The dysgraphia."

She nodded. "I understand, and I'm sorry school was such a struggle for you."

"Football was my escape. The only place where my brain and my body worked together the way they were supposed to. The whole process of getting thoughts onto paper is still difficult. Taking notes was torture. Essays were my personal hell." His laugh was edged with old pain. "My teachers thought I was lazy or stupid, but my parents fought for me and I was finally tested at the end of my junior year."

"That must have been so frustrating," Ella said softly, thinking of her own perfectly organized notebooks and color-coded study guides. Her ease and enjoyment of school.

"Yeah, well. I got pretty good at playing the class clown to hide how much I was struggling. The football team helped. Coach Martinez figured out I learned better through movement and hands-on stuff. Started teaching plays by having us walk through them instead of just drawing them up. Made me feel like maybe I wasn't broken after all."

Ella's heart ached at the matter-of-fact way he described it. "You weren't broken. Your brain just works differently." She smiled wryly. "Unlike me—I was just boring. All studying, all the time. My idea of rebellion was reading novels under my desk during math class."

"Somehow I doubt you were boring. Bet you were cute as hell, sitting there with your secret book and your perfect posture."

"I was not. I was awkward and serious and…" She trailed off as he reached over to tuck a strand of hair behind her ear.

"Sounds adorable to me." His touch lingered for a moment before he pulled back. "So what were you reading under that desk? The classics?"

She laughed. "Hardly. I read steamy romance novels."

"Do tell, Miss McIntyre."

"Ssh, the part with the opossums is coming up," she said but settled closer to him and his warmth.

He let go of her hand but put that arm across her shoulders, pulling her closer to his side. She might have only cautiously poked at her feelings for Ryder as she would have a sore tooth with her tongue, but they were there and growing.

She might almost be that virgin that Cassie had suspected, but she was a woman and knew Ryder was interested in her sexually. But did his feelings go beyond that?

And the biggest question of all: Did she care?

## *Chapter Ten*

The next week passed in a flurry of activity for the carnival. She and Ryder spent time together with the other volunteers but didn't have a lot of opportunities for time alone. She still had her other job at the Dinosaur Center, and he had the ranch to run.

Ella and Millie closed the library early on Thursday afternoon to begin decorating. Ella dragged boxes out of the conference room. Volunteers were scheduled to come in the next morning to put the finishing touches on everything.

"I really appreciate all the hard work you've put into this," Millie told her as they pulled out decorations.

"I just hope it works to get us back on track."

"I met with the library board last night," Millie said.

"Oh?"

"I was going to wait to tell you this, but I may as well go ahead now."

Ella's stomach clenched at Millie's somber tone. Was all this work for nothing?

Millie smiled, putting her hand on Ella's upper arm. "Don't panic. It's good news."

Ella let out her breath. "Don't keep me in suspense."

"I will be retiring next month, and I recommended you for my job as head librarian. The board agreed with me, but there's one caveat."

"Y-yes?"

"You'll be head librarian, but you might also be the only librarian," Millie said and patted Ella's shoulder. "At least until the town gets back on its feet financially. With the new dinosaur place opening at some point and our enthusiastic and capable new mayor, I'm sure that will happen."

"Oh, Millie, thank you. I'm going to miss you, but I will take good care of your library." Ella threw her arms around the older woman and gave her a hug.

"It's going to be your library now, dear, and I know I couldn't be leaving it in better hands."

"Are we celebrating something?" Cassie asked from behind the two women.

"I'm going to be the new head librarian," Ella told her friend.

"Woo-hoo! Congratulations," Cassie shouted. Looking around, she said, "Oops. I need to use my library voice. I hear the new head librarian is strict."

"Who's strict? What's going on?" Ryder came up to them carrying a tool chest.

"Ella is going to be the new head librarian," Cassie said.

"That's wonderful." Ryder set the tool chest down with a thunk and pulled Ella in for a hug. "We're definitely going to celebrate this," he whispered into her ear.

"Okay, you two," Cassie said, poking Ryder in the

back. "We have a carnival to set up so we can save this place for our new head librarian."

Ella laughed as Ryder let her go. "You mean the only librarian."

"Doesn't mean you're not the best," Ryder said and winced when he spotted Millie. "Sorry, Miz Griswold. That's not to say you haven't done a wonderful job over the years."

Millie waved away his apology. "Years is right, and now it's time for me to step aside—and time to get this place decorated."

"Yes, ma'am," he said and picked up the tool chest, heading to the conference room where they'd stored the lumber for the booths.

"Seriously? Who puts Cupid next to a black cat?" Ella was standing on tiptoes atop the library ladder, stretching to hang a glittery red heart beside a construction-paper feline with an arched back.

"Someone who's planning the world's first Valentine's–slash–Friday the thirteenth carnival?" Ryder's deep voice floated up from below, where he steadied the ladder with one hand and held a box of decorations with the other.

"Fair point." Ella stifled a laugh. "But it's going to confuse the children of Tenacity. 'Is love lucky or unlucky, Miss McIntyre?'" She mimicked a child's voice.

"Both," he answered simply. "Love's the luckiest unlucky thing that ever happened to anyone."

His comment brought her back to the opinions he's expressed regarding long-term relationships during their first lunch together. Just because they'd grown closer since then and shared some hot kisses didn't mean he'd changed his mind.

Ella glanced down at him, trying not to notice how his flannel shirt stretched across shoulders built from years of ranch work. She was still torn between wanting him and being realistic about getting physically involved with him. It was probably already too late to guard her heart. And what good was her virtue doing her? She wasn't getting any younger and—

"You don't agree?" Ryder asked, interrupting her thoughts.

Did she? She didn't know the answer, so she challenged him instead. "That's surprisingly profound for a man who once told me his deepest thought was wondering if horses dream about running or just standing around."

"Hey now. That's still a legitimate question."

Why did his eyes have to crinkle at the corners when he smiled? And why did her heart do that flutter thing again—the thing she'd been trying to ignore since the first time he'd smiled at her?

The ladder wobbled slightly, and Ryder's grip tightened. "Careful up there, Ms. Head Librarian."

"I've climbed this ladder a thousand times, cowboy. I could do it in my sleep."

"Please don't."

Ella taped the last heart in place and started down. Halfway to the bottom, her foot slipped on a rung slick with glitter. She gasped—then found herself caught in Ryder's arms, the box of decorations abandoned on the floor.

"You were saying?" One eyebrow raised in that infuriating way of his.

"That I maybe shouldn't climb ladders in my sleep," Ella admitted, her face burning. She was acutely aware of his hands on her waist, her arms around his neck. He smelled like pine and leather and something distinctly Ryder. "You can put me down now."

"I can, but do I want to?" But he lowered her gently, his hands lingering a moment longer than necessary.

"Another surprisingly profound question?" she asked, a bit breathless but not from almost falling.

"Well, I—"

"Hey, hey. No lollygagging, you two. We have to get this place in shape by tomorrow night," Cassie said as she passed them.

"Yes, ma'am," they said at the same time.

Cassie rolled her eyes and went back to the main room of the library.

"I meant it about celebrating your promotion," Ryder said as he picked up the box he'd dropped when she'd slipped.

"I'll hold you to it."

By Friday afternoon, the Tenacity Public Library was unrecognizable. Red and pink hearts dangled from the ceiling. Black cats with arched backs stood guard over book displays. "Broken mirrors" made from aluminum foil decorated the walls alongside lace doilies. The checkout desk boasted both candy hearts and little plastic spiders.

"Mayor Garrett is going to think we've lost our

minds," Ella said, surveying their work. "But I think the fundraiser is going to be a hit."

"It's certainly…memorable," Ryder agreed.

He bent to pick up a fallen heart, and Ella definitely did not notice how his jeans fit. Nope. Not at all.

"You've been a huge help," she said quickly, to distract herself. "I don't think Frank the janitor would have been nearly as enthusiastic about hanging 'Beware of Cupid' signs."

"Frank's sixty-five and hates ladders. And crafts. And probably love."

"Don't forget happiness. He's not a fan of that, either, and he won't be a fan of us if we don't do a good job of cleaning up after ourselves." Ella moved to one of the refreshment tables, arranging heart-shaped cookies beside cups of Love Potion Punch decorated with plastic flies.

"Don't worry. I won't leave until this place is spick-and-span."

"That's sweet, but it might be pretty late. Don't you have to rise early to wrangle cattle or something?"

Ryder leaned against the circulation desk, crossing his arms. "First, we don't 'wrangle' much on a modern cattle ranch. Second, Dad and Noah can cover for me in the morning. Third…" He paused. "Maybe I like spending time with you."

Ella dropped a cookie. "Oh."

"Yeah. Oh." His smile was slow, deliberate.

"But…" Ella frowned. Did he really enjoy spending time with her? She wasn't like all those other women he'd been seen dancing and flirting with.

"But what?"

"I'm boring. I catalog books for fun. I have a spreadsheet tracking every novel I've read since ninth grade." Oh good lord, why was she babbling? The time they'd spent together had been special. "I name wild possums."

"Funny you should mention that. So do I." Ryder picked up the fallen cookie and tossed it in the trash. "Why wouldn't I want to spend time with you?"

"Because the last exciting thing I did before meeting you was reorganizing my spice rack alphabetically."

"In fairness, that does sound boring."

Ella threw a paper heart at him. He caught it deftly.

"But," he continued, "you came with me to the hospital when I was nervous about bringing Harley. You learned how to snowshoe so we could go looking for the aurora. You forgave me for a failed date, patched me up and fed me." He stepped closer. "Nothing about you is boring, Ella McIntyre."

Something warm bloomed in her chest. "You were attacked by that grouse because of— Wait, what failed date?"

"The night I was supposed to take you to a restaurant in Bronco."

"Rescuing that possum was more important." Before she could think better of it, Ella stood on tiptoe and kissed his cheek. "Thank you."

A flush crept up his neck. "If I'd known that was the reward, I'd have stopped for suspected roadkill years ago."

The library door swung open, and Mrs. Potts, the town's oldest resident and most enthusiastic gossip, stuck her head in. Her eyes widened at the decorations—and at Ryder and Ella standing close together.

"Well. Don't you two make a picture. Just decorating, are we?"

"Yes, Mrs. Potts," Ella said quickly, stepping back. "Just getting ready for the carnival. Did you need something? We're closed while we get everything set up."

"Is my daughter-in-law in the back? She asked me to bring some lace doilies."

"Yes, she was in the conference room last I saw her. Remember to bring your grandchildren tonight."

"Oh, I will." The elderly woman's eyes twinkled mischievously. "Though it seems Cupid's already been busy in here." With a knowing laugh, she disappeared down the hall.

"Ella?"

"What?"

He took her hand in his. "Does it bother you that I—"

Before he could finish, the door burst open again. This time it was a group of teenagers from the high school volunteer program, arms full of more decorations.

"Miss McIntyre," called Ruby Matthews. "We brought the 'Lucky in Love' banner and— Oh." The girl stopped short, spotting their joined hands. The other teens giggled behind her.

Ryder let go of Ella's hand but didn't step away. "Perfect timing, kids. We need help with the fortune-telling booth. Who wants to write some Valentine fortunes that are also vaguely ominous?"

"Me!" several voices called at once.

As the teens swarmed in, bringing chaos and energy, Ella found herself watching Ryder directing them, patient and kind even as they teased him about being in the library instead of on a horse. He caught her looking and winked.

Maybe this Valentine's Day would be lucky after all—Friday the thirteenth notwithstanding. She'd have to ask him what he'd been going to ask her before they were interrupted. Was he going to ask if she minded that he didn't ever intend to settle down?

The bigger question was…did she?

•

Tonight, the library hummed with energy as people of all ages wandered between game booths and tried their luck at the Lucky Book raffle. The library had never looked less like itself, and that was exactly what Ella had hoped for. Red and pink paper hearts fluttered from the ceiling, sharing space with black plastic cats. Strategically placed strobe lights made shadows dance across book spines, transforming the usually serene space into something magical and just a touch spooky. The Friday the thirteenth Valentine's carnival was in full swing, and already the crowd was larger than she'd dared to dream.

"Ella." Mrs. Henderson, one of their most loyal patrons, waved from the black cat ring toss. "You've outdone yourself, dear. I must say, mixing Valentine's Day with Friday the thirteenth? I wasn't sure about it at first, but it works."

Ella beamed, adjusting her name tag. "Thanks."

Of course, most of the crowd was gathered around one particular attraction.

Ella's heart did a little flip as she allowed herself to look—really look—at the kissing booth. Or more specifically, at Ryder Trent, who'd somehow managed to make a simple red flannel shirt look like high fashion. The Stetson didn't hurt, either, nor did those boots that added an extra inch to his already impressive height. He'd insisted on the Western theme, drawling something about "giving the ladies what they want."

Judging by the line stretching halfway to the reference section, he'd been right.

"Next up," Ryder called out, and Ella watched as Mrs. Peterson, who had to be pushing eighty, practically floated to the booth, her cheeks already pink. Ryder tipped his hat, those blue eyes of his twinkling. "Well now, darlin', you're the prettiest thing I've seen all night."

Mrs. Peterson giggled like a schoolgirl, dropped her ticket in the jar and closed her eyes. The kiss was quick and sweet but Mrs. Peterson looked as if she'd just experienced true love's first kiss. Ella remembered that feeling from the night they'd gone out in snowshoes to see the aurora.

But that was ridiculous. Ryder looked at everyone that way. It was part of his charm, wasn't it? The ability to make whoever he was talking to feel special.

And Ella wasn't jealous. Nope not one bit.

Ella forced her attention away from the kissing booth. She needed to check out the other booths to be sure everything was running smoothly. But her eyes betrayed her and she glanced over at the Kissin' Cowboy once more, just in time to see him kiss Jenny, who sometimes manned the cash register at Tenacity Feed and Seed. Jenny's hand lingered on Ryder's chest afterward, and something hot and unpleasant curled in Ella's stomach.

Yep. That was definitely jealousy.

"You could always buy a ticket yourself," Millie said quietly, giving Ella a knowing look.

"Don't be silly." Ella busied herself putting out more decorated cookies on the refreshment table, refusing to meet her friend's eyes. "I'm the event organizer. It wouldn't be professional."

"Professional?" Millie snorted. "Honey, this is a small-town carnival, not a board meeting. Besides, I've seen the way he's been looking over at you when you're not watching."

Ella's hands fumbled, scattering cookies across the tray. "I'm sure he wasn't looking at me in any special way."

"If you say so." Millie's tone made it clear she believed otherwise. "Just like you weren't looking at him special just now?"

"I was monitoring the booth's success," Ella protested weakly. "Making sure everything was running smoothly."

"Mmm-hmm. And I suppose you were monitoring his success when you spent twenty minutes watching him set up the booth earlier? Making sure he hung those red curtains just right?"

Heat crept up Ella's neck. Had she been that obvious?

She'd told herself she was just being thorough, checking all the booths equally. But if she was honest, she'd spent far more time watching Ryder's capable hands arrange the decorations than she had supervising any other station. The way his muscles moved under that flannel shirt as he'd stretched to hang the sign…

"Next." Ryder's voice carried across the room, and Ella's heart did that annoying flutter again. She forced herself to look away, to focus on straightening a crooked streamer. She had work to do. A carnival to run. She couldn't spend the whole night mooning over Ryder Trent like every other woman in town.

Even if part of her wished she was brave enough to join that line.

But she didn't want a quick carnival peck, but a proper kiss like that night. The one had made her toes curl and her heart race while the world faded away until nothing had existed but his lips on hers and his hands…

"Ella?" One of the volunteers waved from the craft table. "Do we have any more glue sticks?"

"I'll get some," Ella called back, grateful for the distraction. She had a job to do, and she was going to do it. No more stealing glances at the kissing booth. No more daydreaming about reforming a certain playboy cowboy.

But as she hurried toward the supply closet, she couldn't quite silence the traitorous little voice in her head that whispered, maybe Millie was right. Maybe, just maybe, she wasn't the only one stealing glances when she thought no one was looking.

* * *

After another check of the library to be sure things were running smoothly, Ella helped herself to some punch at the refreshment table. She was aware of Ryder's presence across the room, though she tried to focus on the story one of the local attorneys was telling her about his son. Gideon Frost's brown eyes glowed warmly as he spoke about his boy.

"Where is Scotty?" Ella asked, glancing around to see if she could spot the four-year-old.

"He's with my mom, trying his hand at the black cat ring toss. He seems to think I brought him bad luck at some of the other games."

"We've tried to make it easy for the younger kids to win. I'd hate to have them disappointed."

"Don't worry. He's doing fine. I'll bet he wants his grandmother to buy him some more of those pretzels shaped like the number thirteen."

"I see. He knows Grandma is a mark," Ella said, managing a genuine smile. A divorced single dad, Gideon was quite handsome, solidly built with wavy brown hair and brown eyes. Although Ella had a feeling a lot of people might underestimate the attorney because of his boyish good looks, she had a feeling that would be a mistake. Gideon was her age and a terrific guy, and in other circumstances, she might have found herself drawn to his gentle nature and obvious devotion to his son.

"You got that right," Gideon said with a smile.

Ellis Corey joined them, his campaign-ready charm

still evident in the way he had been working the room. He had run for mayor the previous year.

"Ella, good to see you," he said, touching her elbow briefly. "You should have helped with my campaign."

Ella drew her head back in surprise. "Me?"

"Exactly. Who would have thought to pull together romance and horror?"

Ella laughed. "Some people might think they're one and the same."

She caught a glimpse of Ryder over Ellis's shoulder, his jaw tightening as he watched their interaction. Her heart skipped, but she forced herself to look away.

As she turned back around, she found a cowboy holding out a fresh glass of punch to her. Archer Callahan. The brother of Cassie's fiancé, Graham.

He smiled as she took the punch. "My future sister-in-law speaks very highly of you," he said. "Not only did you pull together this event, but Cassie says you're responsible for her and Graham's lovely weekend getaway."

"I'm not sure it's credit or blame," Ella responded with a laugh, accepting the drink.

Archer joined in with the laughter. "My brother is quite happy, so I'd say credit."

She couldn't help but think about Ryder's opinion on happily-ever-after and spared a quick peek at the kissing booth. This time, their gazes locked. The intensity in his expression made her breath catch—there was something raw and possessive in the way he watched her laugh with these other men. And for a moment, Ella could have sworn she saw a flash of jealousy beneath his usual controlled demeanor.

Was it possible or was she projecting her own jealousy onto him?

Archer looked toward the entrance with a frown. "I don't believe we know the guy in the fancy suit who just walked in. Do you, Ella? He seems to be heading this way."

Ella turned to see who Archer was talking about and frowned. He looked familiar but she couldn't— Oh, the doctor from their visit to the hospital in Bronco. What was he doing here? Sure, he looked nice in his dark suit and loafers, but he stuck out like a sore thumb in a library filled with jeans, flannel shirts and cowboy boots.

"Dr. Tremblay, I'm surprised to see you here," Ella said as he approached.

"It's Rick, please," he said and nodded to the three men who were now surrounding Ella as if to protect her from a fancy-suit- wearin' outsider. "I heard about your little fundraiser and thought I'd drop by."

Ella stiffened. Little fundraiser? Talk about condescending.

*Be nice*, Ella scolded herself and smiled and introduced the doctor to Ellis, Archer and Gideon.

Ella was proud of Tenacity and its residents. They might not be as successful as their neighbors in Bronco but everyone was willing to come together and help one another.

She couldn't imagine living anywhere else. And not just because Ryder Trent called it home.

That was just a perk. Wasn't it?

# *Chapter Eleven*

Ryder stepped back from the Kissin' Cowboy booth and rubbed his jaw. Eight straight hours of puckering up for Tenacity Public Library had left his lips chapped and his patience thin. Not that he'd admit it to anyone—especially not to his sister Cassie, who'd somehow convinced him that his "expertise" in this particular area would be the library's financial salvation.

"Final tally, Kissin' Cowboy." Millie, the head librarian, waved a ledger book around. Her rhinestone reading glasses hung from a beaded chain, and her Valentine's sweater—complete with blinking heart-shaped lights—looked like it had been knitted during the Reagan administration.

"How bad is it?" Ryder tried to peek at the numbers.

Millie slapped the book shut with a wicked grin. "Bad? We have enough to update our computer software, son. That's just your booth. You're a regular one-man stimulus package for literacy."

Ryder managed not to wince at her unfortunate choice of words. "Happy to help the cause."

"'Course you are." Millie adjusted her glasses and peered up at him. "Though I noticed you were checking the clock mighty often once that fancy doctor fella from Bronco showed up."

Yeah, what was he doing here? At first, Ryder couldn't place him but then remembered seeing the man at the hospital when they'd brought Harley to visit the sick kids. He'd bet one or both of his sisters might have had something to do with his appearance here. After all, Renee was the one who had voluntold him to bring Harley to the hospital in Bronco.

"Just making sure I put in my full shift." Ryder grabbed a roll of paper towels and spray cleaner from under the booth and began wiping down the counter, hoping the disinfectant smell would chase Millie away before she could dissect his love life any further.

No such luck.

"Humph." Millie propped her hands on her ample hips. "You put in your shift, all right, but your heart wasn't in those last dozen kisses. Take Bethany Wilson for instance, you pecked her like she was your great-aunt."

"Bethany is my great-aunt, Millie."

"Just checking to see if you knew it." Millie's eyes sparkled with mischief.

Ryder rolled his eyes. He wasn't about to admit that Tenacity's new head librarian-to-be had somehow burrowed under his skin and he couldn't seem to shake her loose.

"You about finished with that counter, or you aiming to wear a hole clean through it?" Millie asked.

Ryder tossed the paper towel in a nearby trash bin and surveyed the nearly empty library. Most of the Valentine's Day and Friday the thirteenth carnival decorations had been packed away. Paper cupids and black cats had been stuffed into storage boxes. All that remained of the carnival was a handful of volunteers and the lingering smell of popcorn and hot chocolate.

And Ella. She stood across the room by the fortune-telling booth, with the Bronco doctor who'd shown up halfway through the carnival and hadn't left her side since.

From this distance, Ryder couldn't make out their conversation, but Ella's laugh carried across the room—a warm, genuine sound that made something twist in his chest. Her blond hair caught the overhead lights as she threw her head back, clearly delighted by whatever the doctor had just said.

"Go help her," Millie prodded.

"Seems like she's got plenty of help."

"Seems like she's being polite to the fella who donated a hefty sum to keep our library's doors open." Millie gave him a gentle shove. "Now quit your bellyaching and make yourself useful. That pompous doc may have a fat wallet, but he doesn't know where the cleaning supplies are kept."

"Yes, ma'am." Ryder surrendered to her logic and made his way across the room, weaving between folded tables and stacked chairs.

As he approached, Dr. Perfect Teeth was gesturing enthusiastically. "—and I told her, I don't care if he is the hospital administrator, no one gets to rush me during a delicate procedure. The nerve suture alone took—"

"Excuse me," Ryder interrupted, directing his words

to Ella though his eyes swept coolly over the doctor. "Millie asked if you need a hand cleaning up your booth. It's the last one to break down."

Ella's expression brightened. "Ryder, perfect timing. Dr. Trem—I mean, Rick, you remember Ryder Trent, one of Tenacity's most successful ranchers."

"And most successful kisser, from what I hear," the doctor said with a smirk. "Five dollars per kiss, was it? I hope you helped Ella save her library."

"It was for charity." Ryder kept his tone even.

Dr. Teeth checked his watch. "Well, I should be heading back. Early rounds tomorrow. I hope you'll think about what I said, Ella."

Ryder busied himself dismantling the fortune-telling booth, keeping his back turned while Rick departed, unwilling to watch in case the good doctor tried to give Ella a kiss. She'd called him a successful rancher, but did she think that more desirable than a doctor? Janelle certainly wouldn't have.

When the library door closed, Ryder turned to find Ella studying him, her head tilted slightly, a small smile playing at the corners of her mouth.

"You planning to take that booth apart with your bare hands, or would you like some tools?" she asked.

He glanced down, realizing he'd been gripping the edge of the plywood structure hard enough to nearly leave marks. "Tools might help."

She disappeared into a storage closet and returned with a cordless drill. "You handle the destruction, I'll pack the props."

They worked in companionable silence for a few

minutes, the quiet of the now-empty library broken only by the whir of the drill and the rustle of tissue paper as Ella wrapped crystal balls and tarot cards.

"So," Ryder ventured, "you seemed to hit it off with the doc."

Ella shrugged, carefully placing a wrapped item in a box. "He made a generous donation."

"And I'm guessing it wasn't out of the goodness of his heart?"

Ella paused, her eyebrows lifting slightly. "What do you mean by that, Ryder Trent?"

"I—" Ryder fumbled. "He said to think about what he said. So I assumed he wanted something."

"Mmm." The sound held a note of amusement. "Well, your assumption is correct. He invited me to some charity gala next month in Bronco Heights."

"And you said?"

"I said I'd think about it." She taped a box closed with precise movements.

"I see," Ryder said through gritted teeth.

"Don't you dare take that tone with me, Ryder Trent."

His head popped up at her fierce admonition. He opened his mouth, but no sound came out.

"I had to stand here and watch you kiss millions of women tonight and—"

"It was hardly millions," he said, finally finding his voice.

"Well, it certainly felt like it."

He stared at her. Was it possible that she'd been bothered by him kissing those other women? "The only woman I truly wanted to kiss tonight never bought a ticket."

She swallowed. So he stepped closer. He thought of their kiss beneath the aurora, how different it had felt from any other. Not just the electricity of attraction, but something deeper—a sense of recognition, perhaps. The feeling that something meaningful was happening, something that might change the course of both their lives if they let it. And it terrified him.

"How about it? It's for a good cause, right?" He regretted the words as soon as they left his mouth. He started to raise his hand as if he could capture those words and pull them back in his fist.

"It's been a long night. I think I need to get home. I didn't put out anything for the possum." She gathered her belongings. "Thank you again for all your hard work."

Ryder rubbed a hand over his face. That sounded like goodbye. His chest tightened, squeezing him so it hurt to breathe. "Ella, I didn't mean it like that."

"Maybe. Maybe not." She headed toward the door. "I promised Millie I'd lock up."

"Of course." He followed. "Do you need a ride?"

She shook her head. "I have my car here."

"I want to be sure you get home safe."

"I have a lot of experience driving in Montana winters."

"Okay. Take care," he said when he really wanted to say a lot more.

The thought left a hollow feeling in his chest. Because the truth was, jealousy wasn't the only thing he'd felt watching her with that fancy-dressed doctor.

He'd felt fear, too. Fear that he might lose something he hadn't fully claimed yet. Something he wasn't sure he deserved.

He stood watching her moving carefully across the snow-slicked parking lot to her car, keys in hand. She was halfway to her car when she stopped and faced him. "I plan to tell him no if he calls."

She turned back and kept walking before he could respond. But he was able to take a deep breath. He didn't need to ask who or what she was talking about.

Ryder started his truck as Ella's headlights cut through the falling snow. He'd spent the last three years avoiding complications, steering clear of anything that threatened to tie him down or make him vulnerable. But sitting there in the empty parking lot, watching Ella drive away, he realized with startling clarity that he was already tied to her in ways he couldn't easily unravel. Already vulnerable in ways he hadn't anticipated.

The question now was whether he had the courage to do something about it. Whether Ryder Trent, reformed heartbreaker of Tenacity, Montana, could risk his heart on a woman who might very well break it.

After leaving out some fruit for Awesome, Ella came back to the kitchen to find her phone buzzing with an incoming call. She picked up the phone, saw that it was from Ryder and paused for a moment.

Connecting the call, she said, "Hey."

"I wanted to be sure you got home safely," he said.

"Thank you, I did." She leaned against the kitchen counter.

"I also wanted to apologize for that crack about the kiss being for a worthy cause. I acted like an ass, and I'm as sorry as I can be."

"Because you didn't get a kiss?" she asked. Was that what this was about? Or was he giving her a true apology?

"Because I hurt your feelings. I don't deserve a kiss, but I still want one."

She shifted her weight against the counter, unable to stay angry with a contrite Ryder. At least he was owning up to his comment and realized that it had hurt her. "Tonight?"

"As tempting as that sounds, how about tomorrow night?" he asked, his tone unmistakably hopeful even over the phone.

"Tomorrow is Valentine's Day." Was he actually asking her out on the biggest date night of the year?

"I was thinking we could go to supper and then the annual dance at the community center."

"You don't have a date for Valentine's Day?" She found that hard to believe.

"No. Do you?"

"No." She couldn't remember the last time she had a date for Valentine's.

"Then maybe you'll let me take you out?"

She swallowed. Maybe that had been just a careless remark, a forgivable one. "I'd like that, but you know they're predicting snow."

"It's winter in Montana. They're always predicting snow," he said on what sounded like a sigh of relief.

They chatted a bit more about the successful carnival and then agreed on what time he'd pick her up the following evening. After hanging up, Ella looked around her kitchen, but all she was seeing was Ryder as he looked tonight.

She might be setting herself up for heartbreak, but if so, it was already too late. Her heart was already involved.

Ella's heart raced when she spotted Ryder's truck pulling into her driveway the next night. She opened her front door as he walked up the short sidewalk to her home. He looked spectacular in dark pants and a charcoal button-down, his boots freshly polished. In one hand, he carried a bouquet of winter roses in deep crimson and soft pink. In the other, rather unexpectedly, was a paper bag from Tenacity Grocery.

"Happy Valentine's Day," he said, hanging on to the flowers and presenting the bag with a flourish

She gave him a puzzled grin and pulled out a container. "Grapes. How thoughtful."

"Oh," he said with mock disappointment. "I was going to give these to Awesome, but would you rather have these?" he asked, handing her the flowers.

"The grapes are lovely, but I think Awesome would prefer them. If that's okay with you?"

He briefly bowed his head. "I defer to your wisdom regarding opossums."

The Tenacity Town Hall had undergone its annual Valentine's Day transformation: Crepe-paper streamers in varying shades of pink and red crisscrossed the ceiling of the ordinarily utilitarian space, while twinkling white lights outlined the windows, casting a warm glow that softened the harsh fluorescent overheads.

"Reckon this is about the fanciest I've seen this old place look since last February," Ryder said as they stood in the doorway. They'd enjoyed dinner at Castillo's, and Ella was glad the evening still had a long way to go.

His mellow baritone sending an involuntary shiver down her spine had nothing to do with the February chill. His usual scent of leather and fresh air was now mingled with something spicy—aftershave, she realized. He'd made an effort tonight.

"Amazing what some dollar store decorations and community spirit can accomplish," she replied, her voice steadier than her pulse.

"You look different tonight. I've been trying to put my finger on it," he said, his eyes making a quick sweep from head to toe and back.

"Different good or different strange?" Ella asked before she could stop herself.

A small smile tugged at the corner of his mouth. "Good. But you always look good."

"I'm wearing makeup and I ditched my glasses for tonight. So I hope I don't have to read anything," she said with a self-conscious shrug.

"I like your glasses."

"You do?"

He touched the tip of her nose. "Very librarian. I have this fantasy," he said and glanced around.

"Don't you dare," she said with a roll of her eyes, but she spoiled it with a giggle.

From across the room, Daniel Taylor's voice carried above the music as he leaned toward Mike Cooper. "Weather service is saying eight inches, maybe more by morning."

"That's what they said last year," Mike replied, adjusting his lapel, "and we barely got a dusting."

Ryder's attention remained fixed on Ella. "Thirsty?" he asked, nodding toward the punch bowl.

"If it's the same punch as last night's carnival, I know exactly how much sugar went in there. My teeth are protesting just standing near it." She smiled. "But don't let me stop you."

"Never developed much of a sweet tooth." His eyes held hers a moment longer than strictly necessary. "Dance floor's filling up. Shall we?"

The fluttering in her stomach intensified. Time for a confession. "I should have warned you ahead of time. I'm not much of a dancer," she said, suddenly aware of how the dress she'd ordered online might look under the twinkling lights. What had seemed festive and daring in her bedroom mirror now felt like an invitation for the entire town to notice she wasn't the same old Ella tonight.

"Just follow my lead," Ryder said.

She hesitated for a moment, thinking about all the gossip she'd heard about him dancing with various women at the Grizzly Bar. Before she could chicken out, Ella placed her hand in his outstretched one. His palm was warm and callused against her softer skin, a contrast that somehow felt exactly right.

As they made their way to the dance floor, Winter Hernandez-Sanchez nudged her husband, Luca. "Look there. Told you something was brewing between those two."

Luca followed his wife's gaze. "Librarian and the rancher? Huh." He shrugged. "Hope he doesn't track cow manure on her books."

"Luca, you've got all the romance of a fence post," Winter scolded, though there was no real heat in it.

Ryder looked at Ella and grinned at the exchange between the Sanchezes. She smiled back, uncaring what anyone in Tenacity thought. Nothing was going to spoil this evening.

Listening to the banter between the Sanchezes eased Ella's awkwardness as she and Ryder found a rhythm together. His hand settled more confidently at her waist, and Ella allowed herself to step a fraction closer than strictly necessary. The scent of his aftershave wrapped around her like a promise.

"Town looks good on you," he said after a comfortable silence, his voice pitched low enough that only she could hear.

Ella tilted her head. "What does that mean, exactly?"

"You fit here. Some folks try to make Tenacity into something it's not. You make it better just by being yourself in it."

The simple observation struck her with unexpected force. Her own parents had been trying to get her to leave and use her education somewhere else. Arguing that she'd fit better elsewhere.

"That might be the nicest thing anyone's said to me in a long time," she replied honestly.

"As you probably already know, I'm not much for

flowery talk," Ryder said, his thumb tracing a small, perhaps unconscious circle against the fabric covering her lower back. "But I notice things."

"What else do you notice?" The question slipped out before she could censor it.

His eyes darkened slightly. "That you shelve the romance novels with extra care. That you keep peppermints in your desk drawer but never eat them yourself. That when you laugh—really laugh—you get this little crinkle right here." His gaze dropped briefly to the corner of her mouth.

Heat bloomed in Ella's cheeks. "I didn't realize I was quite so transparent."

"Not transparent. Just…worth paying attention to."

The song transitioned seamlessly into another slow number, and neither made any move to leave the dance floor. Ella found herself relaxing into his hold, her hand shifting from his shoulder to rest against the solid warmth of his chest. Beneath her palm, his heartbeat seemed to quicken.

"Folks're saying we're in for a real Montana special tonight," said Howard Jenkins as he and his wife, Margaret, two-stepped past them. "Better not linger too long after the party."

Margaret swatted her husband's arm. "Don't you mind Howard. He's been predicting the storm of the century every winter since '98."

"Been right once or twice," Howard protested good-naturedly as they danced away.

Ryder and Ella exchanged amused glances but said nothing, content in their small bubble of warmth in the chilled February night. The rest of the town hall seemed to recede, the music wrapping around them like a cocoon.

"Our snowshoe adventure last week," Ryder said suddenly, his voice dropping even lower. "Been thinking about it."

Ella's breath caught. The all-too-brief kiss had replayed in her mind countless times. "Me, too," she admitted.

"Been thinking maybe we could try it again sometime. Gotta keep practicing with the snowshoes if you want to become proficient."

"Did I say I wanted to become proficient?" she countered, tilting her face up to his. "Maybe I considered it a medieval form of torture."

"Really?"

"At first, but the rewards far outweighed the following day's muscle aches."

Something shifted in his expression—a hunger quickly banked behind careful restraint. The hand at her waist tightened almost imperceptibly.

"Is that right?" His voice now had a roughness to it that made her pulse skip.

Around them, the dance floor had grown more crowded as nearly everyone at the party joined in. Through the windows, Ella caught glimpses of fat, lazy snowflakes beginning to drift down from the night sky. The forecast that had been background noise all evening suddenly seemed more significant.

"Looks like the weather folks might be right for once," she said, nodding toward the window.

Ryder didn't turn to look. "Let it snow," he said simply.

They danced together right up until the band announced their last song. Glancing around, Ella realized that she and Ryder were alone on the dance floor.

"I guess it's time to leave," she said.

"Mmm," Ryder murmured and took her hand.

They collected their coats and went into the February night.

"Beautiful," Ella breathed, watching the pristine white blanketed the parking lot and the surrounding pines.

"Sure is," Ryder agreed, though when she turned, she found him looking at her rather than the snow.

The moment stretched between them, fragile and expectant. Ella's gaze dropped to his mouth, remembering the pressure of his lips against hers the week before. The look in his eyes now promised he'd take the lead. And she was willing to go where he led.

"About that kiss," he said, his voice a low rumble that seemed to vibrate through her.

"I believe in action over words," she said, surprising herself with her boldness.

His smile was slow and devastating. "Yes, ma'am. I believe you do."

He stepped closer, one hand coming up to cup her cheek. The callused pad of his thumb brushed across her lower lip with exquisite gentleness, raising goose bumps along her arms despite the warmth of her coat. When his mouth finally met hers, Ella sighed into the kiss, her hands finding purchase on the solid strength of his shoulders.

This kiss was nothing like the first—hesitation replaced by certainty, brevity by lingering exploration. His arms encircled her fully, drawing her against the firm wall of his chest as though he'd been waiting to hold her properly for far too long. Ella's fingers slid into hair that curled at the nape of his neck, reveling in its softness against her skin.

When they finally broke apart, they remained close, sharing breath in the small cloud of warmth they'd created in the cold night air. The snow continued to fall around them, heavier now, muffling the sounds of the cleanup crew inside.

His eyes met hers and he brushed another, briefer kiss against her lips. "Reckon we ought to head home before this snow gets any ideas about stranding us here."

The reluctance in his voice matched the feeling in her chest. Their evening felt unfinished somehow, this new evolution of their relationship too fresh to be interrupted by practical concerns like weather and road conditions.

"I suppose," she agreed without enthusiasm. She didn't want the evening to end.

Behind them, the snow continued to fall, blanketing Tenacity in a pristine white cover that promised to transform the familiar landscape by morning. But for Ella, the real transformation had already begun, right here on this February night. The future suddenly felt full of new possibilities.

# *Chapter Twelve*

Ryder could barely see past the hood of his truck. The snow was coming down faster now, collecting on the windshield quicker than the wipers could clear it away. What had started as light flurries when they'd left the Valentine's dance had transformed into something far more serious in the span of twenty minutes.

He glanced over at Ella, who'd gone quiet after chattering happily about the dance for the first part of their drive. Her hands were folded in her lap, and he caught the slight worry in her profile as she stared out at the increasingly treacherous conditions.

"You doing okay over there?" he asked, tightening his grip on the steering wheel as the truck slid slightly on a patch of ice. The back tires fishtailed before he corrected their course.

Ella turned to him with a smile that didn't quite reach her eyes. "Sure. Just…concentrating on the weather, I guess."

"Makes two of us." Ryder leaned forward, as if those extra few inches might help him see through the white curtain obscuring the road ahead. "I should've checked the forecast more carefully before we stayed so late."

"Don't be silly. Neither of us knew it would get this bad this fast."

"Howard Jenkins did," he muttered.

"He's always predicting some sort of disaster. And I didn't see him rushing out of there."

He appreciated her saying that, but it didn't ease the knot of responsibility tightening in his chest. This was technically their first official date, though they'd been spending time together for weeks between planning for the carnival and the other excuses he'd thought up to spend time with her. Tonight was supposed to be perfect. He'd even bought her favorite chocolates but had second-guessed himself and left the heart-shaped box in the truck when he picked her up.

The headlights barely penetrated the swirling white void ahead. The normally familiar stretch of county road between the town hall and the turn toward Ella's place had become alien territory. Ryder slowed to a crawl, hunching forward.

"Maybe we should go back and wait it out," Ella suggested softly.

"We're closer to your place than turning back. I think we can make—"

The flash of movement came from nowhere—a panicked deer materializing directly in their path, eyes reflecting the headlights like twin moons. Ryder's body reacted before his mind had time to process. He cranked the wheel hard to the right, the truck's tires losing purchase on the slick road. They slid sideways, the world spinning in a blur of white until they came to an abrupt halt with a soft crunch as the passenger side sank into a snowbank.

For a moment, neither of them spoke. The only sound was the idle of the engine and the rhythmic sweep of wipers clearing snow nobody could see through anymore.

Ryder's knuckles had gone white against the steering wheel. He couldn't seem to loosen his grip even though they'd stopped moving. His pulse hammered in his ears like a stampede.

"You okay?" he finally managed, forcing himself to look at Ella.

To his surprise, she looked calmer than he felt. "I'm fine. Are you?"

"Yeah." He finally pried his fingers from the wheel, flexing them to restore circulation. "God, Ella, I'm so sorry."

"For what? Saving that deer's life and probably ours, too?" She shook her head, blond waves bouncing against her shoulders. "That was some impressive driving."

"Some impressive driving would've gotten you home without ending up in a ditch," he muttered.

"Stop that." Her voice was gentle but firm. "This wasn't your fault, Ryder. It's a snow squall."

He turned off the engine and unbuckled his seat belt. "Let me check the damage."

When he pushed against his door, the wind nearly ripped it from his grasp. Snow blew sideways into the cab, stinging his face like tiny needles. The squall had intensified to near-whiteout conditions.

"Ryder, wait!" Ella called over the howl of the wind.

She reached across and grabbed his arm, her touch warm even through the sleeve of his dress shirt. "Let it pass first. This can't last long."

Logic told him she was right. He reluctantly pulled the door shut, sealing them back inside the warm cab. Snow had already dusted the console between them and melted into dark patches on his pants.

"I should call for help." He pulled out his phone, then frowned at the screen. "No service."

"Typical Tenacity," Ella said with a wry smile. "I swear this town has more cellular dead zones than actual zones."

Despite everything, Ryder found himself smiling back. That was something he'd noticed about Ella McIntyre early on—her ability to find humor in situations that would leave others cursing under their breath. Especially some of the women he'd dated. It was part of what drew him to her, that and the way her eyes lit up when she talked about books, or how she'd named that opossum who'd taken up residence behind her house "Awesome" because, as she put it, "He's living his best life and isn't apologizing to anyone."

Ryder ran a hand through his hair, trying to push away the feeling of having failed her somehow. "I had plans, you know. Dinner at Castillo's followed by the dance. Taking you home…"

"Plans are overrated," Ella said. "Sometimes the universe has better ideas."

"Being stuck in a snowbank was the universe's better idea?"

"We're protected in here from the snow, we're safe

and…" She turned in her seat and peered into the back. "And if I'm not mistaken, is that a heart-shaped box of chocolates back there?"

She started to reach into the back but stopped abruptly. "Unless…unless you bought those for some other—"

"Absolutely not!" he interrupted. "I had you in mind when I bought them."

She swallowed audibly. "Well, that's good to know, anyway."

Warmth crept up Ryder's neck. "I, uh, didn't want to overdo it earlier. I already had the flowers and those grapes for Awesome."

"You brought grapes for my opossum…" Her smile widened. "And then worried about overdoing it?"

"Well, when you put it that way…"

"Hand over those chocolates, cowboy. Turns out they were good planning after all."

He reached back and grabbed the red box, passing it to her with a self-conscious shrug. "Nothing fancy. Just those dark truffles you mentioned liking that time at the library."

Ella's expression softened as she took the box. "You remembered that? I was just rambling while we worked on the carnival."

"I listen when you ramble." The admission came out more earnest than he'd intended.

She busied herself with opening the box, hiding whatever reaction might have crossed her face. "Want one?" she asked, holding the open box toward him.

"Ladies first."

"Such a gentleman." There was a teasing note in her voice as she selected a chocolate and took a delicate bite. Her eyes closed briefly, and the small sound of pleasure she made sent an unexpected jolt through him.

They sat munching chocolates in companionable silence for a while, the tension in Ryder's shoulders gradually easing. Outside, the snow continued its relentless descent, but somehow it seemed less threatening now. The truck was still warm despite the engine being turned off, and Ella's presence beside him was a comfort he hadn't known he needed.

Ella was anything but comfortable. Oh, the truck was warm enough, and the chocolate was delicious, but sitting just inches away from Ryder while trapped in this intimate bubble was doing terrible things to her composure. If she'd thought dancing with him had been a test of willpower, this was pure torture of the sweetest kind.

She sneaked a glance at his profile—the strong line of his jaw now dusted with stubble, the way his dark blond hair curled slightly at the nape of his neck, those capable hands that managed to be both strong and gentle at the same time. Hands she'd been imagining on her skin for weeks now, if she was being honest with herself.

The truck suddenly felt several degrees warmer.

Ella reached for the radio dial, needing something—anything—to break the charged silence. "Mind if I find some music?"

"Go ahead," Ryder said, his voice somehow lower than before.

She turned the knob, skipping past static until a clear signal emerged. A plaintive country melody filled the cab, Anne Murray singing about wanting their dance to last forever. Ella immediately regretted her choice but couldn't bring herself to change it without drawing attention to the lyrics about falling in love while dancing.

Great. Just perfect. Could the universe be any less subtle?

She risked another glance at Ryder, who seemed suddenly fascinated with wiping the condensation that had built up on the driver's side window. His jaw was tense, and something in his manner had shifted.

"This is awkward, isn't it?" she blurted, immediately wishing she could recall the words.

His eyes met hers, surprised. "What?"

"Being stuck here. With me. I'm sure you'd rather be trapped with someone else. Someone more your…type." The words tasted bitter even as she said them, but some masochistic part of her needed to hear him confirm that this unlikely attraction was one-sided.

To her surprise, Ryder laughed. It wasn't a dismissive sound, but something warmer, edged with disbelief. He shook his head. "My type?"

"You know what I mean."

"I really don't, Ella." He shifted in his seat to face her more directly. "What exactly do you think my 'type' is?"

She waved a hand vaguely. "I don't know. Someone like Brianna Collins or Sophia Miller. The women I've seen you with around town."

"Brianna moved to Bozeman, and Sophia wanted to sell me hay for the ranch."

"Oh." Ella felt her cheeks warm. "I didn't know that."

"Clearly." His eyes, the color of blue flames, studied her with an intensity that made her heart skitter. "The truth is, I'm trying real hard to be a gentleman right now, and it's proving to be something of a challenge."

The implication of his words hung in the air between them. Ella's pulse quickened as she processed what he was saying.

"A gentleman," she repeated carefully.

Ryder ran a hand across the back of his neck, a gesture she'd noticed he made when uncomfortable. "Look, Ella, I like you. Have since you chewed me out for shelving that Louis L'Amour book in the wrong section."

"You put it in romance," she protested. "The man wrote Westerns."

A smile tugged at his mouth. "And you were passionate about it. That's the thing about you—you care about stuff. Really care. Even in a struggling small-town library. It's...appealing."

"Appealing," she echoed, feeling slightly dazed. Was this conversation really happening?

"Yeah." His gaze dropped briefly to her lips, then back to her eyes. "Very."

Understanding dawned with a rush of heat that had nothing to do with the truck's heater. All this time she'd been assuming he was just being friendly, that their interactions were nothing more than being polite to his sister's friend. Meanwhile, he'd been...what? Holding back?

"Ryder," she said, surprising herself with the steadiness in her voice, "maybe you're being a little too much of a gentleman."

Those blue eyes darkened further. "Ella—"

"I'm serious." She held his gaze, letting him see the truth in hers. "I don't need gentlemanly right now."

For a heartbeat, neither of them moved. Then Ryder shifted, closing the distance between them in one fluid motion. His hand came up to cradle her face, thumb brushing her cheekbone with a gentleness that contradicted the heat in his eyes.

"You sure about this?" he asked, his voice a low rumble that she felt more than heard.

In answer, Ella leaned in and pressed her lips to his.

For a moment, Ryder went still against her, as if shocked by her boldness. Then he made a sound deep in his throat and took control of the kiss, turning it from tentative to consuming in the space of a heartbeat. His hand slid from her cheek to tangle in her hair, angling her head to deepen the contact. His lips were firm but gentle, coaxing responses from her she hadn't known she was capable of giving. When his tongue traced the seam of her lips, she opened to him without hesitation, meeting his exploration with her own.

The kiss escalated quickly, weeks of shared glances and careful conversations distilling into something urgent and needy. Ella's hands found their way to his shoulders, feeling the solid strength beneath his dress shirt. She shifted, trying to get closer despite the center console between them.

Ryder broke the kiss, both of them breathing hard.

"Back seat would be more comfortable," he suggested, voice rough.

Ella nodded, not trusting her voice. Discarding their coats, they awkwardly maneuvered over the seats into the more spacious rear of the extended cab. No sooner had they settled than Ryder pulled her into his lap, his hands spanning her waist as he claimed her mouth again.

The new position eliminated the barriers between them. Ella could feel the hard planes of his chest against her, the unmistakable evidence of his desire beneath her. She shifted experimentally, drawing a groan from him that sent a thrill through her.

His hands slid up her sides, thumbs brushing the undersides of her breasts through her dress. Even that slight contact sent sparks racing along her nerves. When his mouth left hers to trace a path down her throat, she let her head fall back, giving him better access.

"God, Ella," he murmured against her skin. "You have no idea how long I've wanted this."

She rolled her hips against him, delighting in his sharp intake of breath. "Show me."

His hands found the zipper at the back of her dress, pausing there. "You sure?"

In answer, she reached between them and began unbuttoning his shirt, revealing tanned skin and the dusting of dark hair across his chest. Ryder's restraint seemed to snap. He tugged her zipper down in one smooth movement, his warm hands sliding beneath the fabric to caress her bare back.

The feeling of skin against skin was electric. Ella

arched into his touch as his hands moved to her front, cupping her through the thin material of her bra. When his thumb brushed across her nipple, she gasped.

"Sensitive," he observed with a smile she felt against her throat.

"Only with you," she admitted, then immediately felt foolish. "I mean—"

Ryder drew back, studying her face. "What do you mean?"

Heat that had nothing to do with desire flooded her cheeks. "Nothing. I just… It's been a while for me."

Something shifted in his expression. "How long is 'a while,' exactly?"

"Um." She bit her lip. "College?"

His hands stilled on her waist. "College? But that's… You graduated, what, four years ago?"

"Five," she corrected, wishing the seat would swallow her whole. "Is that a problem?"

"No," he said quickly. "Not at all. Just…um…surprising."

She disentangled herself from his lap, suddenly self-conscious. "It's not that surprising. I've only been with one guy, okay? And it was…disappointing."

Understanding dawned in Ryder's eyes. "First times can be less than stellar."

"It wasn't just that it was my first time," she clarified, tugging her dress back into place and reaching for her discarded coat. "He made me feel like it was my fault. Like I was doing it wrong, or there was something wrong with me."

"That guy was a world-class jerk, then." Anger flashed

across Ryder's features. He reached for her hand, his touch gentle. "Because that kiss? Spectacular."

A small smile tugged at her lips despite her embarrassment. "You've had a lot more experience than me. I might be disappointing."

"Ella." The way he said her name made her look up. "First off, I'm hardly Casanova. I've had relationships, sure, but I don't sleep around. I like to know a woman before things get…intimate."

"And do you? Know me?"

His expression softened. "I'd like to think so. We've been circling each other for weeks now. And while this might technically be our first conventional date, it doesn't feel that way, does it?"

She had to admit it didn't. From their first meeting, there had been an ease between them that defied the usual awkwardness of new acquaintances. "No, it doesn't."

"I want you to know something," he said, brushing hair from her face. "This, us—it means something to me. It's not just…" He gestured vaguely at their disheveled state.

"It means something to me, too," she whispered, and was rewarded with a smile that made her heart flip.

"Good." He pressed a gentle kiss to her lips, then drew back with visible reluctance. "Which is why I don't want our first time together to be in the back seat of my truck."

Disappointment warred with the warmth his words kindled in her chest. "Oh."

"Don't get me wrong," he added quickly, "I want

you. More than I've wanted anyone in a long time. But you deserve better than this."

"What if I don't want better? What if I just want you?" The boldness of her statement surprised even her.

Ryder groaned, resting his forehead against hers. "You're killing me, Ella McIntyre." He took a deep breath. "But I think we should slow down. Before we can't."

Part of her wanted to argue, to pull him back to her and damn the consequences. But the bigger part appreciated his restraint, his concern for making their first time together something more than a frantic coupling born of circumstance.

"Okay," she agreed softly.

They stayed like that for a moment longer, foreheads touching, sharing breath. Then Ryder pressed a kiss to her temple and straightened, buttoning his shirt with fingers that weren't quite steady.

As if on cue, Ella noticed the change in the quality of light around them. The furious wind had died down, and through the windows, she could see individual snowflakes drifting down rather than the impenetrable white wall from before.

"Looks like the squall's passed," she observed.

Ryder followed her gaze. "About time it went to terrorize some other part of Montana."

They clambered back into the front seats, both of them a little shy now as they straightened clothing and smoothed hair. Ryder started the engine, testing the truck's response. To their relief, it backed out of the snowbank without much difficulty.

The rest of the drive to Ella's place passed in comfortable silence. Ryder kept both hands firmly on the wheel this time, but occasionally shot her glances that made her skin warm despite their agreement to wait.

When they pulled into her driveway, he came around to open her door, ever the gentleman despite what had transpired between them. The night air was crisp and cold after the warmth of the truck, snowflakes catching in her hair as they walked to her porch.

At her door, Ella turned to face him. "Aren't you coming in?"

Something like regret flickered in his eyes. "It's been a long night. Rain check?"

The words sent a chill through her. Had he changed his mind? Now that he knew how inexperienced she was, had he decided she wasn't worth the trouble after all?

"Sure," she said, fighting to keep her voice casual. "Whenever."

Ryder must have read something in her expression, because he stepped closer, one hand coming up to cup her cheek. "I meant what I said, Ella. This means something to me. I just think we both need a little time to… process."

She wanted to believe him. But doubt, that old companion, whispered that she'd probably never see him again—at least not like this. He'd find excuses, keep their interactions casual and public. The town of Tenacity wasn't big enough to avoid someone entirely, but it was plenty big enough to keep a comfortable distance if you wanted to. Even if he was Cassie's brother.

"Of course," she said. "Good night, Ryder."

He hesitated, then leaned down to press a soft kiss to her lips. "Sweet dreams, Ella."

She watched him walk back to his truck, his broad shoulders dusted with snow, and tried to quiet the voice in her head that insisted this magical night had been nothing more than a fluke—a product of adrenaline and close quarters that would evaporate in the harsh light of day.

As his taillights disappeared down her driveway, Ella touched her fingers to her lips, still feeling the phantom pressure of his kiss.

Only time would tell if what had sparked between them in that snowbound truck was the beginning of something real or just another disappointment to add to her meager collection of romantic experiences.

Either way, she thought as she unlocked her door and stepped into the quiet darkness of her home, she wouldn't regret tonight. Some memories were worth the risk of heartbreak.

Her biggest regret was that this morning she wasn't wearing something from that secret second drawer in her grandmother's highboy. As she had been last night.

## *Chapter Thirteen*

The next morning, Ella had just finished brushing her teeth when the doorbell rang. Her heart leaped into her throat. Who could be at her door at seven in the morning? She glanced down at her pink flannel pajamas covered in tiny sleeping cats, then shrugged. Whoever it was would have to deal with her comfort-first morning attire.

The bell chimed again, followed by an enthusiastic bark that made her pause halfway down the stairs. That sounded exactly like…

She pulled open the door to find Ryder on her front porch, looking unfairly gorgeous in faded jeans and a navy henley under his trademark shearling jacket. Harley wagged his tail furiously at her feet. In one hand, Ryder held a cardboard drink carrier with two coffee cups. In the other, a paper bag that bore the familiar logo of the Silver Spur Café

“Morning,” he said, a sheepish smile playing at the corners of his mouth. “I, uh, brought breakfast.”

Ella blinked at him, certain she was still dreaming. Just mere hours ago, he couldn’t wait to escape after what had to be the most perfect first date of her life.

And now here he was again, bearing caffeine and sugar. Last night she'd despaired of ever seeing him again.

"This is crazy, isn't it?" Ryder ran a hand through his hair, messing it up in that way that made half the women in town swoon. "I couldn't sleep. Kept thinking about you, about last night. About how I wanted to see you again. So I took Harley for his morning walk and somehow ended up here."

She looked out the door into the driveway. "Isn't that your truck?"

"Harley insisted on a ride after his walk." He laughed softly. "I can go if—"

"Yup, it's completely wacky," Ella cut him off, grabbing his jacket and pulling him inside. The coffee cups wobbled precariously. "Absolutely bonkers."

Then she was in his arms, and his mouth was on hers, and the paper bag crinkled between them as he backed her against the hallway wall. Harley bounded past them into the living room, evidently embarrassed by the behavior of the humans, but Ella couldn't focus on anything except the taste of Ryder's lips and the solid warmth of his body pressed against hers.

"I got chocolate glazed," he murmured between kisses. "And those maple-bacon ones you said you liked."

"Never mind the doughnuts," she breathed, sliding her hands into his hair.

He chuckled against her mouth, then pulled back just enough to set the coffee and bag on the hallway table. When he turned back to her, his eyes had darkened to the color of storm clouds.

"God, you're beautiful," he said, tracing her cheek with his thumb. "Even in flannel pajamas with bed head."

"Last night I had my sexy stuff and no bed head," she lamented, trying to ignore the way her heart fluttered at his words.

But the way he was looking at her now—like she was rare and precious and fascinating—made those rumors about his playboy ways feel distant and unimportant.

"I think these pj's are kinda sexy," he said, then kissed her again, deeper this time, his hands sliding down to her hips to pull her closer.

Ella had dated before. She wasn't completely inexperienced. Just almost. But nothing had prepared her for the way Ryder made her feel, like every nerve ending in her body was sparking to life. Like she was burning up from the inside out. Like she might actually combust if he stopped touching her.

His lips traced a path down her neck, and she gasped, clutching his shoulders. "Ryder…"

"Tell me to stop," he whispered against her skin. "Tell me this is too fast."

"Don't you dare stop."

He groaned, lifting her easily in his arms. "Bedroom?"

"Upstairs, first door on the right," she managed, wrapping her legs around his waist as he carried her up the stairs.

Some distant part of her brain reminded her that she hadn't made her bed, that her sexy underwear drawer remained untouched this morning, that this wasn't how she'd imagined their first time would be. But then Ryder laid her down on her rumpled sheets with infinite tenderness, looking at her like she was everything he'd ever wanted, and none of those things mattered anymore.

"You're sure?" he asked, hovering above her.

In answer, she pulled him down to her, reveling in his weight, his warmth, the way he seemed to surround her completely.

What followed was beyond anything Ella had experienced before. Ryder was patient, attentive, learning her body with careful focus. He whispered praise against her skin, told her how perfect she felt, how he'd dreamed of this. And when they finally came together, the connection was so intense it brought tears to her eyes.

Afterward, as they lay tangled in her sheets, Ryder traced patterns on her bare shoulder. "I know what people say about me," he said quietly. "About my dating history."

Ella tensed slightly. Here it was—the moment where he'd tell her this was fun but not to expect anything serious.

"But I've never felt like this before." He pressed a kiss to her temple. "Never showed up at someone's door at seven a.m. because I couldn't bear not seeing them. Never wanted someone the way I want you."

She rolled over to face him, searching his eyes for any sign of insincerity. But all she found was raw honesty and something that looked remarkably like hope.

"The straitlaced librarian who was practically a virgin?" she asked, only half joking.

"The brilliant, beautiful, sexy-as-hell-in-flannel-pajamas librarian," he corrected. "Who is no longer an almost-virgin."

"Ryder..." She swallowed hard. "I don't want to be just another story people whisper about in the library."

"You won't be." He cupped her face in his hands. "Give me a chance to prove it to you. Let me take you to dinner again tonight. And tomorrow. And the next night. Until you believe me when I say you're different. Special. The only one I want."

The smart thing would be to protect her heart. To remember his reputation and all the broken hearts he'd left in his wake. But as Harley's happy bark echoed up from downstairs, Ella found herself smiling.

"Okay," she whispered. "But you better not be lying about having those maple-bacon doughnuts. And your dog better not have helped himself."

His answering laugh was full of joy and promise. "I brought him a special bone, but those bacon ones are probably getting cold downstairs. Want me to grab them?"

"In a minute." She pulled him close again, marveling at how right this felt. How perfectly they fit together. "I'm not done with you yet."

He laughed. "Insatiable?"

"Well... I..."

He dipped his head and kissed her. "Well, so am I."

And the dance started all over again until they lay exhausted and satiated on her bed.

The late-afternoon sun cast long shadows across the ranch as Ryder guided his truck down the familiar road leading home. His lips still tingled from Ella's kiss, and the scent of her lingered on him despite the shower they'd taken together. He grinned. Maybe that shower was why her scent was still on him. He couldn't remember the last time he'd felt this light, this…happy. But reality came crashing back as he pulled up close to the house and spotted Cassie's car in the driveway. Not totally surprising, since both he and Cassie still lived with their parents in the ranch's main house.

He barely made it through the back door that led into the kitchen before his sister's voice cut through the quiet. "Really, Ryder? Ella?" Cassie stood in the kitchen, arms crossed, her expression a perfect mirror of their mother's disapproving face—the one they'd grown up dreading.

"Not now, Cass." He headed for the fridge, grabbing a beer more for something to do with his hands than any real thirst.

"Yes, now." She followed him, undeterred. "She's my friend. One of my best friends. What were you thinking?"

"I was thinking it's none of your damn business." The bottle cap pinged against the counter as he flicked it off with more force than necessary.

"It became my business when you decided to mess around with someone I care about." Cassie's voice rose. "You don't exactly have the best track record with relationships, in case you've forgotten."

The beer turned bitter in his mouth. "How did you even know I was with her?"

"Because she's the only person I know of in Tenacity

that likes those maple-bacon doughnuts," she said with a shudder. "Howard Jenkins said you were first in line at the Silver Spur to buy them, and Mary Ellen Parker was at the grocery store saying she saw your truck first thing this morning in Ella's driveway."

Damn small-town snoops.

"I told you Ella was different. You spend your weekends at the Grizzly Bar, flirting with every single woman there. You bring different women to family functions so often we take bets on if it will be someone new or a repeat."

"As I said, it's no one's business but mine who I date," he snapped, even as a voice in his head whispered that his sister wasn't entirely wrong. He set the bottle down hard enough that foam surged up the neck.

Cassie's face softened slightly. "I just don't want to see Ella hurt. She doesn't talk about it, but I know some jerk hurt her bad in college."

Ryder fisted his hands. He'd like to get ahold of that guy. "She told me."

Cassie's eyes widened. "She did?"

"Not the whole story, but enough." And she'd also whispered, *I don't want to be just another story people whisper about in the library.* Why had he thought he could prevent that? He knew about his reputation in this town and people were bound to talk. If his own sister didn't trust him…

"Ry…"

"Don't." He held up a hand. "Just…don't."

The kitchen fell silent except for the ancient refrigerator's steady hum. Through the window, he could see the setting sun painting the pasture in shades of gold and purple. A perfect evening for riding fence, losing himself in simple, honest work. Instead, he was here, feeling like his skin was two sizes too small.

"It's different with her," he said finally, voice rough. And that terrified him more than all the gossip and sideways looks combined.

"I'm relieved to hear that."

"But I thought you didn't approve."

"I don't approve of you treating Ella like another casual thing. But if you're serious about her..." Cassie sighed. "Look, maybe instead of assuming you know what Ella *deserves*, you could try asking her what she *wants*."

The suggestion hung in the air between them. Outside, a horse nickered softly from the barn, reminding him of all the work still waiting. Simple work. Safe work. Nothing like the complicated mess of feelings churning in his chest.

"I need to check on the horses," he muttered, heading for the door. But he paused with his hand on the knob, glancing back at his sister. "I'll figure it out, Cass."

"You better." Her voice followed him onto the porch. "Because if you hurt her, I'll have to kill you. And then I'll have to ask her to help me hide the body. And she'll help, because that's what best friends do."

Despite everything, he found himself smiling as he crossed the yard. The familiar scents of hay and leather welcomed him into the barn's shadowy interior, but for once, they brought no peace. His mind kept circling back to Ella—her laugh, the way she saw right through his carefully constructed walls, how she made him want things he'd convinced himself he didn't deserve.

He was in way over his head. And for the first time since Janelle left him bitter and humiliated, he wasn't sure he wanted to swim back to safer shores.

Ella McIntyre brushed a wayward strand of hair from her face and tucked it behind her ear as she reorganized the children's books she'd chosen for the future display at the Dinosaur Center. The winter sun streamed through the small window of the trailer, casting long shadows across the floor and illuminating dust motes that danced in the golden light. She'd spent the better part of an hour going over her plans for the center's educational programs, but her mind kept wandering like a restless colt in a new pasture.

The night with Ryder still clung to her skin like the lingering scent of him. The memory of his callused hands tracing paths across her body made her cheeks flush, and she busied herself with straightening books that didn't need straightening. The quiet of the trailer usually brought her peace, but today it left too much room for her thoughts to echo.

"I reckon those books are about as straight as they're gonna get without using a level," came a voice from behind, startling Ella from her reverie.

Lynda Slater stood in the doorway, her tailored blazer and pencil skirt looking as out of place in Tenacity as a penguin in the desert. The attorney carried a leather portfolio case in one hand and a travel mug of coffee in the other. Despite her polish, there was something approachable about the woman.

"Lynda, hello. I didn't realize you were still here." Ella smiled, grateful for the distraction from her own circular thoughts. "Did the board meeting wrap up already?"

"Thankfully." Lynda set her portfolio on a nearby table and took a sip of coffee. "Thought the chairman would talk us into the next century before we could adjourn."

Ella laughed. "That man never met a five-minute update he couldn't stretch to twenty."

"The curse of small-town governance everywhere." Lynda's shrewd eyes seemed to take in Ella's distracted demeanor. "You seem a million miles away today. Everything all right with the education program?"

"The program's fine." Ella moved to the desk, shuffling papers that didn't need shuffling. "Just a lot on my mind, I guess."

"Would that 'a lot' happen to be about six foot two, wears a Stetson and helps run the Stargazer Ranch?" Lynda's lips quirked upward knowingly.

Ella's head snapped up. "Good lord, does absolutely everyone in this town know my business?"

"You should know that gossip in travels across Tenacity faster than Homer Smith's racing pigeons." Lynda shrugged unapologetically. "I know stuff I don't even want to know, like which town councilman is sleeping on his couch after forgetting his anniversary."

"And here I thought librarians had the market cornered on information networks." Ella sighed, leaning against the desk.

"Honey, lawyers and librarians are cut from the same cloth—we both traffic in other people's stories." Lynda settled into a chair. "So… Ryder Trent, huh?"

The flush crept back into Ella's cheeks. Pride demanded that she say, "It's not serious."

"Your face tells a different story."

Ella busied herself organizing pencils in a mason jar. "What exactly are people saying?"

"Oh, the usual. That the town's notorious playboy has set his sights on the town's librarian. And I don't mean Millie Griswold. And his truck was parked outside your place before the sun was up. That he bought you maple-bacon doughnuts at the Silver Spur and for some reason he's been buying lots of fresh fruit at Tenacity Grocery after asking what opossums eat. I confess that one totally escapes me."

Each detail made Ella's heart do a ridiculous little flip, which only irritated her more.

"Well, whatever they're saying, it's…complicated." Ella sighed, finally abandoning the pretense of work and settling into a chair across from Lynda. "Complicated…isn't that a cliché?"

"Depends. Complicated meaning…?"

"Meaning I'm not sure where I stand." The confession felt both terrifying and liberating. "Everyone knows Ryder's history. He's dated half the eligible women in three counties, and none of them lasted more than a couple months."

"And you're wondering what makes you different," Lynda finished for her.

"Exactly." Ella's fingers found the edge of her sleeve, worrying at a loose thread. "That night was…perfect. But today, I woke up thinking about all the other women who probably felt the same way before reality set in."

"Can I offer some unsolicited advice from someone who's been around the block a few times? And I offer this free of charge. Pro bono." Lynda crossed her ankles in a ladylike gesture that seemed at odds with her direct gaze.

"At this point, I'd take advice from the center's skeletal remains if they weren't still in the ground."

Lynda laughed. "Fair enough. Here's my two cents—you're overthinking it."

"That's my specialty."

"Not everything lasts. That's a fact, but if you spend all your time worrying about the end, you won't enjoy the good stuff. Take it from me. Not all relationships are meaningful, and that's okay."

The weight of those words settled in the quiet room. Ella had never thought of it that way—that her protective instincts might actually be robbing her of present joy.

"So you're saying I should just…what? Pretend I don't care if it ends badly?"

"I'm saying you should embrace your inner goddess, Ella. Enjoy that ride for as long as it lasts." Lynda's blue eyes sparkled with mischief. "Not every relationship needs to be your forever. Sometimes they're just supposed to be fun."

"But what if I'm already past that point?" The question emerged smaller than Ella intended. "What if I'm already in love with him?"

There. She'd said it out loud for the first time, and the world hadn't ended. The sun still slanted through the windows, painting golden stripes across the floor.

"Oh, honey." Lynda's expression softened. "That's a whole different kettle of fish, isn't it?"

Ella nodded, unable to trust her voice.

"Then I'll amend my advice. Be honest. With yourself and with him." Lynda leaned forward, her elbows on her knees. "The worst pain comes from the lies we tell ourselves."

"That sounds like something you'd find cross-stitched on a pillow," Ella quipped, but there was no real bite to her words.

Lynda rose and grabbed her coffee mug and portfolio. "And with that, I gotta run. Good luck, and remember, whatever happens, enjoy the ride. Life's too short to spend it projecting past hurts and what-ifs onto present possibilities."

After Lynda left, Ella sat thinking about her advice.

She stood and gathered her things in preparation to leave but paused at one of the displays that was currently leaning against the floor—a freshly completed plaque describing the hadrosaur.

Ella paused, studying the picture of the ancient creature. Millions of years ago, it had roamed these lands, living its dinosaur life without any concept of the future or the past. No anxiety about tomorrow, no regrets about yesterday. Just fully present in each moment.

Ella's phone dinged with an incoming text, and she pulled it from her purse.

It was Ryder. Are you free for dinner? Say Castillo's at six?

We need to talk so dinner sounds perfect. See you then, she typed, taking a deep breath as her thumb hovered over the send button. Finally she sent the text.

She waited to see if there would be a response, but her phone remained silent. Maybe she shouldn't have said that part about needing to talk. Didn't that scare off guys?

If that was going to scare him off, then so be it. Squaring her shoulders, Ella slipped on her coat and left the trailer, the brisk Montana air enveloping her as she stepped outside.

Whatever happened with Ryder—whether it lasted a season or a lifetime—she would be present for every moment of it. No more letting old wounds dictate her future. It was time to be as brave with her heart as she'd been with every other aspect of her life.

The road ahead might be uncertain, but Ella McIntyre wasn't trying to map it all out in advance. Sometimes you just had to trust the journey.

## *Chapter Fourteen*

Castillo's Mexican Restaurant buzzed. The place was unusually crowded for a Monday night. The smell of sizzling fajitas and the gentle clinking of margarita glasses created a backdrop that should have felt festive. Instead, Ella found herself gripping her water glass a little too tightly, her knuckles whitening as she tried to decipher the look on Ryder's face.

The candlelight between them flickered, casting shadows that made his expression even harder to read. Yesterday she'd been in his arms, her head tucked perfectly into the hollow of his shoulder as if that space had been carved just for her. She'd fallen asleep after their lovemaking and had woken to his lips on her forehead and his hand tracing lazy patterns on her bare back. Now, something had shifted.

She'd sensed it the moment they'd sat down—a new distance in his eyes that hadn't been there when he'd whispered her name.

"So," he finally said, pushing his half-eaten enchilada around his plate. "I've been thinking."

Just like "we need to talk," the words he'd just uttered never led anywhere good. Ella's stomach clenched, but she lifted her chin slightly, determined not to show how much her heart rate had just accelerated.

"About?" She managed to keep her voice steady, impressive considering the circus her insides had become.

Ryder set down his fork and met her eyes directly. "I know things between us moved pretty fast. And I wanted to say that it's okay if you're having second thoughts about the two of us."

Ella blinked, momentarily thrown. Second thoughts? Her thoughts had been firmly in the first-thought category—specifically, wondering if what they had might actually be building toward something real.

"We haven't known each other very long," he continued, "and our relationship began under, well, unusual circumstances."

The "unusual circumstances" being his sister dragging him into the library to volunteer him for the kissing booth at the carnival. It hadn't been the meet-cute she'd imagined for herself, but it had been theirs.

"So if you're not sure about us," Ryder said, his voice oddly formal, "we can part as friends."

The words landed like ice water. Part as friends? Was that what he thought she wanted?

"I see," she said, because she didn't know what else to say. Her mind raced, trying to catch up with what was happening. Was this his move? The whole "let's part as friends" routine? For all she knew, he trotted it out with every woman he dated when he was ready to move on.

Not that she could verify that theory. It wasn't as if she could poll the women of Tenacity who'd previously dated Ryder Trent. The playboy cowboy's reputation preceded him, but she'd foolishly believed their connection might be different.

Apparently not.

"Is that what you want?" she asked, hating how vulnerable the question made her feel.

Ryder's eyes darted away, fixing on something over her shoulder. "I just want to make sure you don't feel... trapped in anything. I know you were worried about gossip, and there seems to be a lot of that going around."

Pride rose in Ella's chest, straightening her spine. She'd be damned if she'd let him see how much this hurt. This man had cradled her face in his hands and kissed her like she contained all the answers to questions he'd never even thought to ask. He'd held her as if he was afraid she might disappear. And now he was serving her this practiced, polite dismissal.

"I had fun with you, Ryder," she said, impressed by her own casual tone. "And I hope you don't regret the experience."

His eyes snapped back to hers, something like surprise flickering in their depths. "No regrets," he said, his voice oddly rough. "Not a single one."

"Good." Ella smiled, the expression feeling brittle on her face. "I should probably get going. Early day at the library tomorrow."

She reached for her purse, determined to make it at least to her car before the tears came.

Ryder watched Ella gather her things, her movements precise and controlled. He'd expected...what? Tears? Arguments? Pleas? Instead, she'd accepted their end with a composure that left him feeling oddly hollow. So much for Cassie's "ask Ella what she wants" suggestions.

*It was there for all to see. Proof that I'm doing the right thing.*

But if it was the right thing, why did it feel like he'd just taken a hoof to the chest?

"Let me walk you to your car," he offered, already reaching for his wallet to settle the bill.

"That's not necessary." Her smile didn't reach her eyes. "I'm perfectly capable of finding my way."

"I know you are." That was part of the problem. Ella McIntyre was perfectly capable of everything. She had a master's degree in library science. She worked at the Dinosaur Center and ran reading programs for kids. She could discuss everything from ancient mythology to the diet of wild opossums.

She was magnificent. And sooner or later, she'd realize that a cowboy with dirt under his fingernails and nothing but a high school diploma to his name wasn't enough for her. The fact that she'd never actually said anything like that didn't matter. It was only a matter of time before she did. Just like Janelle.

Better to end it now, before he got in any deeper. Before he got used to the sound of her laughter first thing in the morning. Before he started imagining a future where that sound was his to wake up to every day.

Too late. He was already in too deep, drowning in the scent of her body wash and the quiet dignity with which she was walking away from him.

"Take care, Ryder," she said, pausing at the edge of their table.

"You, too, Ella."

He watched her walk away, her blond hair catching the light as she passed beneath each hanging lamp. Every step she took toward the door felt like another rib cracking open. Was it supposed to hurt this much? Doing the right thing?

When the door swung shut behind her, Ryder slumped back in his seat.

*Is it, though? How can the right thing hurt so much?*

Later that week, the Grizzly Bar was jumping. Neon beer signs cast a multicolored glow over the crowded dance floor where couples two-stepped to the country band's cover of an old Garth Brooks song. Four weeks ago, Ryder would have been right in the middle of it all, spinning some pretty young thing around the floor, buying drinks and flashing the smile that had earned him his reputation.

Tonight, he was slouched at the bar nursing his second beer and feeling about as lively as a fence post.

"Well, don't you look like something the cat dragged in," Noah said, sliding onto the stool beside him. "Thought you were getting back in the saddle tonight."

Ryder gestured vaguely toward the dance floor. "Just taking a breather."

His brother followed his gaze to where Melissa Hargrove was casting hopeful glances their way. She'd been dropping hints all night, and the old Ryder would have already had her pressed against him on the dance floor. The new Ryder couldn't muster the energy to care.

"Uh-huh," Noah said, ordering a beer for himself. "You've been 'taking a breather' for the last hour. Since when does Ryder Trent sit out half the night?"

"Maybe I'm getting old."

"Or maybe you're finally growing up."

Ryder shot his brother a look. "What's that supposed to mean?"

"Just that I never thought I'd see the day when my brother wouldn't be jumping at the chance to charm the boots off every woman in the bar." Noah took a long pull of his beer. "So what happened between you and the librarian? You have a fight?"

"Nothing happened." Ryder spun his bottle between his palms. "It was never going to last. It's a good thing I ended it when I did."

Noah snorted. "Right. That's why you're sitting here looking like someone shot your dog."

"I'm fine."

"You're a dummy is what you are."

Ryder couldn't argue with that. "She deserves better."

"Better than a hardworking man who treats her well and makes her laugh? Because that's what I've seen these past few weeks." Noah shook his head. "You're not dumb, Ryder. And you're damn sure good enough for anyone in this town, including Ella McIntyre."

Ryder stared into his beer, wishing it held the answers he needed. "Then what's my problem?"

"You're not brave enough," Noah said simply.

The words stung because they rang true. Ryder Trent, who'd broken three ribs riding a bull named Widowmaker on a dare and once jumped into a flooded creek to save a neighbor's child, was terrified of whatever it was he felt when Ella looked at him with those soft blue eyes.

"It's different with her," he admitted quietly.

"No kidding," Noah laughed. "I figured that out the first time I saw you two together at the carnival. You look at that woman like she hung the moon."

"That obvious, huh?"

"To everyone but you, apparently."

The band switched to a slow song, and more couples filled the dance floor. Ryder watched them, wondering if Ella was at home right now, if she was thinking about him at all or if she'd already filed him away under "mistakes not worth repeating."

"I really messed up, didn't I?"

"Yep," Noah agreed cheerfully. "But the good news is, you're still breathing, which means you've got time to fix it."

When Ryder finally dragged himself home later that night, Harley didn't even greet him at the door. The dog cast him a single disapproving look from his bed by the fireplace, then pointedly turned away.

"Not you, too," Ryder groaned.

Harley huffed and settled deeper into his bed.

Even the dog knew he'd screwed up.

Ella shelved the last of the returned books, finding a small satisfaction in the perfect order of the Dewey decimal system. If only human emotions could be so neatly categorized and arranged.

Since that night at Castillo's, she often found herself reaching for her phone to text Ryder whenever she saw something that would make him laugh. She'd deleted his number from her contacts but couldn't seem to delete the memory of his callused hands on her skin or the way his eyes crinkled at the corners when he smiled.

"You're pathetic, McIntyre," she muttered to herself, sliding a copy of *Pride and Prejudice* into place. At least Elizabeth Bennet had the satisfaction of rejecting Mr. Darcy before he could reject her. Ella had just sat there and accepted Ryder's dismissal with a poise she'd been proud of at the time but now felt like a missed opportunity.

She should have thrown her water in his face. Or told him exactly what she thought of men who couldn't commit to anything more substantial than a one-night stand. Or admitted that she'd been falling in love with him, just to see the panic in his eyes.

Instead, she'd smiled and walked away, and now she was left with this hollow ache that made even her beloved books seem dull and lifeless.

Ella's phone buzzed and she jumped to check it. She'd been doing that ever since that night.

"Ella? Do you have a minute?" Lynda Slater asked when Ella answered.

"Of course," Ella said, grateful for the distraction.

"I'm out here at the Dinosaur Center with Grayson Abernathy. They're finalizing plans for the lunar eclipse event and he wanted to discuss a sensory-friendly workshop idea with you."

The Dinosaur Center had become Ella's refuge these past weeks. Between her regular job at the library and her part-time work at the center, she'd barely had time to think, which was exactly how she wanted it.

"I'll head over this afternoon," she promised.

Later, sitting across from Grayson in one of the trailers at the center, Ella found herself actually engaged in the conversation for the first time in days. Grayson told her that his family—especially his dad, Vernon, and his grandfather Raymond—had encouraged his passion for science even as he followed his other passion, ranching. And now he wanted to make sure it was accessible to all children. His fervor was infectious, and his ideas for a sensory-friendly dinosaur workshop ahead of the eclipse event were thoughtful and creative.

"We could set up a quiet zone where kids who get overwhelmed can take a break," he was saying. "And maybe some hands-on fossil stations with different textures."

"That sounds perfect," Ella agreed. "I know several kids on the spectrum from the library and the community center programs, and they would love something like this."

Grayson smiled. "I was hoping you might help run it. The kids all adore you."

"I'd be honored," she said, meaning it.

They spent another hour working out the details, and by the time they finished, Ella realized she hadn't thought about Ryder once. Well, until now so it was a small victory, but she'd take it.

"This has been great," Grayson said as they gathered their notes. "You know, I was wondering if maybe you'd like to grab dinner sometime? No pressure, just thought it might be nice to talk about something other than fossils for a change."

Ella looked at him, genuinely caught off guard. At forty, Grayson was be a bit older than she but he was definitely attractive with his blue eyes and brown hair. And those broad shoulders filled out his shirts quite nicely.

"I—" she started, then paused. It would be easy to say yes. She couldn't imagine Grayson breaking her heart over enchiladas.

But it wouldn't be fair to him.

"I'm flattered," she said carefully. "But I'm not in a good headspace right now."

Understanding dawned in his eyes. "Ah. Heart troubles?"

"Is it that obvious?"

"Only to someone who's been there." He smiled ruefully. "Can I offer some unsolicited advice?"

"At this point, I'll take advice from anyone, solicited or not."

"Don't waste time on someone who won't invest in intimacy. Life's too short to love people who keep parts of themselves locked away."

Ella opened her mouth to object, because that wasn't really fair to Ryder. For all his faults, he had shared intimate parts of himself with her. He'd told her about how he'd struggled with his dysgraphia, about his dreams for the ranch, about the horse he'd raised from a foal that had died suddenly last spring and how he'd cried like a baby over it.

Before she could voice any of this, movement at the office door caught her eye. She looked up—and there he was. Ryder Trent, looking rumpled and uncertain, his Stetson clutched in his hands.

"Sorry to interrupt," he said, his eyes locked on Ella's face like a man who'd been wandering in the desert catching his first glimpse of water.

Ryder had nearly talked himself out of coming at least five times on the drive over. But after two weeks of sleepless nights and one particularly pointed conversation with his brother, he'd finally worked up the courage to find Ella and beg for another chance.

Now, watching her deep in conversation with Grayson Abernathy, he felt his heart sink. The rancher and autism coach was leaning toward Ella, his expression earnest, and she was looking back at him with what appeared to be genuine interest.

*Too late*, Ryder thought with a stab of despair. *I waited too long.*

Grayson looked up, spotted Ryder and smoothly rose to his feet. "I should get back to the teachers to let them know about the special sensory workshops," he said to Ella, gathering his papers. As he passed Ryder in the doorway, he paused. "You were a lucky man and didn't even know it. Now, be brave," he said quietly, then continued down the hall.

Ryder stared after him, Noah's accusation of cowardice echoing in his ears. He took a deep breath and stepped into the office.

"Hey," he said, eloquence failing him completely.

"Hey yourself," Ella replied, her expression guarded.

Ryder cleared his throat. "I owe you an apology."

"For what?"

"For a lot of things but especially for breaking up with you."

Ella's eyebrows rose slightly. "We hadn't made any commitments to each other, Ryder."

It wasn't a jab, merely a statement of fact, which somehow made it worse. Because she was right. He'd never said the words out loud, never made any promises.

"Maybe not," he admitted. "But the moment I held you in my arms, I felt like I was yours."

Confusion flickered across her face, followed by understanding. "Right." She nodded slowly. "You don't want to be committed to anyone."

"No, that's not—" Ryder ran a hand through his hair in frustration. "I don't want to be committed to just anyone. I want to be committed to you. Only you." He swallowed hard. "I am committed to you. I have been since that that night we went snowshoeing. Heck, probably even before that. I just…got overwhelmed by all the feels."

"All the feels?" Ella repeated, a hint of something—amusement? hope?—in her voice.

"Yeah," Ryder said, feeling his face heat up. "Turns out there are a lot of them where you're concerned."

"You could have just told me that instead of pushing me away," Ella said, and for the first time, he heard the hurt beneath her composed exterior. "You broke my heart, Ryder."

The words hit him like a physical blow. "I'm sorry," he said, meaning it more than any apology he'd ever given. "I don't know why I did that."

But even as he said it, he realized that wasn't quite true.

"Or maybe I do," he admitted. "My ex, Janelle—she used to say I lacked ambition because I didn't want to leave Tenacity or get a degree. That I was wasting my potential being 'just' a rancher."

Ella's expression softened slightly. "I never said anything like that. Nor did I think it."

"No, you didn't. None of this was your fault. It was all up here." He tapped his temple. "I know most people don't take me seriously. But I'm content with my life. Working the land, taking care of the animals—it's a good life. An honest one."

"I know that," Ella said. "And I'd never want you to be anything other than who you are."

Hope flickered in Ryder's chest. "I was afraid of losing myself somehow. Of not being enough. But these days, and nights, without you have been hell. When I thought about never holding you again, it made me crazy."

He moved closer, not quite touching her yet, afraid of being rebuffed. "When Noah accused me of being a coward, I couldn't even argue. Because he was right. I was scared of how much I..." He swallowed. "Of how much I love you."

The words hung in the air between them.

"Hold up," Ryder said suddenly, realizing she hadn't actually agreed to anything. "I'm sorry. You have a say in all this. What do *you* want, Ella?"

She looked at him for a long moment, her blue eyes searching his face as if looking for something specific. Then her expression softened, and she held out her arms.

"I want my cowboy back," she said simply.

Ryder didn't need to be told twice. He crossed the room in two strides and pulled her into his arms, dropping fervent little kisses all over her face, each one punctuated with a whispered "sorry."

"I'm sorry… I'm so sorry… I love you… I'm sorry…"

Someone cleared their throat loudly, and they jumped apart like guilty teenagers. Lynda Slater stood in the doorway, shaking her head but grinning from ear to ear.

"Pay no attention to my previous advice," she told Ella. "Clearly I was wrong. Sometimes fun does turn into forever."

"What's she talking about?" Ryder asked as Lynda disappeared out the door.

Ella laughed, the sound warming him from the inside out. "I'll explain later," she promised. "Much later."

Ella's place was hers—but the moment Ryder stepped through the door, it felt more like home than the ranch house where he'd grown up. How would she feel about him moving into her place? The ranch wasn't all that far. He could live here and still work the ranch.

Before he could ask, he spotted a bag of opossum

feed on her kitchen counter and smiled. He was pretty sure she'd be agreeable. Easier than trying to relocate a wild animal.

Later, much later, they lay tangled in her sheets, Ella's head on his chest and his fingers tracing lazy patterns on her bare skin. Outside, the Montana night was clear and cold, stars scattered like diamonds across the velvet sky.

"I love you," he whispered into the darkness, no longer afraid of the words or what they meant. "I'll never hurt you again, Ella. I'll spend the rest of my life keeping you safe and warm and protected, if you'll have me."

She lifted her head to look at him, her eyes soft and full of something that made his heart ache with happiness. "Of course I'll have you. I love you, too, you stubborn cowboy."

Ryder reached over to the nightstand and pulled open the drawer, extracting a small velvet box. He'd bought it three days ago, after a long conversation with his father about courage and second chances.

"Ryder?" Ella's eyes widened as he placed the box between them.

"I know it's fast," he said. "But I also know what I want. And that's you, for the rest of my days."

He opened the box to reveal a simple diamond set in white gold, nothing flashy but solid and true.

Ella stared at the ring, then at him. Suddenly, she snapped her fingers. "Oh darn," she said, her expression falling.

Ryder's heart stuttered. "What's wrong?"

A slow grin spread across her face. “I wasn’t wearing anything from my satin and lace drawer.”

Relief washed over him, followed by a burst of laughter. “We have the rest of our lives for that,” he promised, taking the ring from its box.

“You know,” she said carefully, “we don’t have to take any big steps if marriage still spooks you.”

Ryder pressed his fingers gently against her lips, shaking his head. “We’re getting hitched as soon as possible,” he said firmly. “I want Tenacity—heck, the whole world—to know you’re mine and I’m yours. Forever.”

As he slid the ring onto her finger, Ryder Trent finally understood what his father had always told him about finding the right woman. It wasn’t about giving up who you were. It was about becoming more—more yourself, more whole, more alive—because you’d found the person who made you brave enough to love without fear.

And if there was one thing the people of Tenacity understood, it was the value of holding on to what mattered, no matter how hard the journey. After all, that’s why they called it Tenacity in the first place.

# *Epilogue*

"Ssh," Ella said. "You need to keep quiet, but it's only for a minute, I promise. I heard Ryder's truck in the driveway."

She closed the cover on the box despite the whining and snuffling coming from inside. "I know. I know. But it's not for long."

She patted the box. Today was their wedding anniversary, and she'd gotten her husband a special present. The word *husband* still gave her a thrill, and she grinned.

Harley had gone back to his owner, Liam Martin. As much as she understood it was the right thing for him, it was one of the hardest things they'd had to do. Harley belonged with his owner, but his absence had left a big whole in their lives.

So Ella had jumped at the chance when Renee had contacted her about a lab-mix puppy that needed a home. She also had another surprise for Ryder, but she'd deal with the rambunctious puppy first.

"Ella?" Ryder called out as he came into the house. His boots dropped onto the floor by the door with a thump.

For now, they still lived in her 1920s Sears catalog home.

"In here," she called from the kitchen, not wanting to move the box.

Ryder appeared in the doorway, and Ella threw her arms around him and plopped a loud kiss on his lips. "Welcome home."

He kissed her back. Pulling away, he licked his lips. "Hmm, maybe I should go out so I can come back in."

She laughed and swatted his arm. "I have a gift for you."

"A gift?"

"For our anniversary," she told him.

"Oh, was that today?"

"It is, and just for that maybe I should keep the gift."

Ryder glanced over her shoulder. "I think your gift is trying to make a break for it."

She turned around to see the box swaying back and forth and finally landing on its side. "Oh dear."

She squatted down and opened the box. Pulling out the wriggling puppy, she rose and handed it to Ryder. "Happy anniversary."

He looked surprised and a bit uncomfortable. Not the reaction she was going for.

"You don't like it?" she asked, deflated by the reception her gift was getting.

"I love it," he said and kissed her, not easy while trying to avoid a puppy tongue. "But I have something for you, too."

He handed the puppy back to her and hightailed it into the living room.

He came back holding a squirming puppy—a different one! "Happy anniversary, Ella."

She burst out laughing.

"You're not angry?" Ryder asked.

They exchanged puppies and laughed as the animals nipped and kissed their faces.

"So, should we keep both?" Ryder asked in a hopeful voice.

"Of course. Like you said, kids and dogs go together."

"Kids and…?" He stared at her for a moment. Blinking, he said, "Does that mean…?"

"It sure does. I took a home test a little while ago."

He put his puppy on the floor and reached out, took hers from her arms and set it on the floor. Picking Ella up in his arms, he twirled her around the kitchen, the puppies chasing, yapping and jumping.

"You realize our lives are going to be crazy from now on," Ella said as he gently set her down.

"And I'm going to love every minute of it," he said. "I love you, Ella Trent."

"And I love you, Ryder Trent. Forever."

"Forever," Ryder agreed and glanced down. "Uh-oh. I think one of the puppies just peed."

"Yeah, and it was yours, so you get to clean it up," Ella said with a laugh.

* * * * *